THE WEDDING DEBT

CLARISSA WILD

ONE

Jill

Age 9

Once upon a time, there was a girl with a crown too heavy for her head and a prince who was ready to steal it all for himself.

"No, give that back!" I scream as Luca runs past me and snatches the crown right off my delicate head.

He laughs out loud and spins around on the grass a few feet away from me, dangling the crown between his index finger and thumb while wearing a disgusting smirk on his face. He blows aside a strand of his brown hair, his dark eyes taunting me. "C'mon then. I dare you to get it back."

My eye twitches, and my hand curls into a fist. "Give. It.

Back," I say through gritted teeth.

When I approach him, he keeps backing up, making it impossible to retrieve.

"Stop," I hiss.

"No," he replies, grinning so broadly I want to take off these pretty new heels I got from Mom and jab them in his face.

Instead, I dig my heels in and sprint toward him, trying to catch him off guard. He twirls the crown around right as I catch up, giggling hard as he sidesteps to avoid me. "Missed," he muses.

I growl in frustration. "Luca!"

"Jill!" He imitates my voice with a high-pitched tone, and the sound makes my blood boil.

"C'mon, Luca …" My sister, Jasmine, sighs as she follows us around the garden in her pink dress.

"What, *Jasmine*?" he scoffs.

"It's not funny!" I jump to snatch the crown from his hand, but he keeps throwing it up and down, out of my reach, backtracking like he enjoys seeing me struggle.

So I stop and put my hands against my side. "Why do you do this? Huh?"

He raises a brow and shrugs. "Because you look stupid."

My jaw drops, and a gasp escapes my mouth. "I do not!"

"Only queens and princesses wear crowns," he retorts. "And you're neither."

I'm fuming so much it feels like steam might exit from my ears. "I *am* a queen!"

4

He waggles a finger. "Queens are only queens if they're married to a king." He plops the crown onto his own head. "Maybe I'll be one now."

Jasmine begins to giggle, but when I look at her, she slaps her hand in front of her mouth like she's trying to hide it.

"C'mon then, Jill. You wanted to be a queen," Luca jests, and he waves his hand and dips into a bow.

I frown. "What? You want me to be *your* queen?" I snort out loud.

He cocks his head. "A queen isn't a queen if she isn't married."

I revolt at that thought.

Me marrying Luca? No way.

I turn away from him, sticking my nose up into the air. "I would rather marry a slug than you."

"A slug?" He laughs himself silly to the point of losing the crown.

I continue to ignore him while Jasmine approaches me. "Let's do something else."

"No, I want my crown back." I'm standing my ground. "He can't bully me."

Luca slowly approaches us. He's still holding the crown with a look full of mischief on his face. I don't trust him, but maybe I'll be able to steal it away again if he gets close enough.

"I'll give it back …" he mutters.

I turn and look at him, holding out my hand.

But instead of handing me the crown, he hands me a slug.

I shriek out loud and drop the slug, scraping my hand along my dress to get rid of the slime it left. Luca is laughing so hard he can't catch his breath.

"That isn't funny!" I yell, stomping my feet.

"Yeah, it is," he responds, still laughing while pointing at me. "Your face."

Now I turn even redder, like a volcano ready to explode.

"Luca, c'mon," Jasmine says, sighing out loud. "Stop."

When she tries to snatch the crown from his hand, he quickly jumps back again, still taunting us. He just can't get enough of teasing us, and I hate it.

"It's just a crown. Why do you care so much?"

"Why do *you*?" I retort.

He shrugs. "Who plays dress-up anyway?"

"We like it," Jasmine responds.

"What's there to like? Dumb clothes," he says. "Don't make you any less ugly."

My jaw drops. "Ugly!?"

Jasmine sticks out her tongue. "Girls play better than boys anyway."

"Not," he quips.

I try to snatch the crown again when he's distracted by Jasmine, but it isn't working. He's much bigger than I am, and it's making me so angry.

"You won't get it back," he says as I jump around him.

"Why not?" I say.

"I think I'll keep it." He lowers it and puts it onto his own head again. "See? Looks much better on me than it could ever look on you."

"Oh, please," I respond, crossing my arms. "If you wanted to play with us, you could've just said so."

"No way." He wanders off to pick up a stick from the ground that he uses to whack the long strands of grass. "Annoying you is way more fun."

With a sigh, I watch him walk off with an essential piece of my outfit. "Why do you always have to be such an ass?"

"Yeah, Luca, why are you such an ass?"

His older brother, Liam, suddenly pokes his head out from the front door. He's the same age as Jasmine, just a few years older than me, but much more handsome with those flowing dark locks of hair. He watches us with a smile on his face as though he finds it all super funny like Luca.

We've been playing in the yard while our parents were busy talking, and for some reason, they wanted Liam to stay inside while we were shooed outside. But now that he's finally joining us, maybe Luca won't act like such a stupid kid.

"Hey, Jasmine!" Liam says, smiling broadly, but Jasmine just looks away, completely embarrassed.

"Really?" Luca yells at Liam, kicking a rock. "No one asked you to meddle, Liam."

"What did he do this time?" Liam asks as he walks up to me, ignoring his brother.

"Jasmine and I were just playing dress-up, and then

Luca stole my crown," I respond.

He smiles at me and then waves at Luca. "Give it back to her, Luca."

I smile at him, tucking my hair behind my ear. "Thank you."

Liam has always been so nice to me, unlike his younger brother, Luca. I can't stand that annoying kid. I mean, he is my age, but he acts like he's older and tougher, and I don't know why, but I don't care either.

Luca ignores him, still whacking around that stick like it's a sword or something.

Liam puts his hands against his face. "Luca!"

Luca throws him an angered look.

"Mom and Dad won't like this."

Luca pauses for a moment and then chucks the stick far away. He walks toward us but pauses halfway through the grass … only to snatch the crown off his own head and send it hurtling through the air. The crown lands only a few inches away from my feet.

Luca's arms span wide. "Happy now?"

Liam signals him with his hand, and I say another, "Thanks," in his direction.

"Oh, I don't get a thanks?" Luca scoffs, raising his brow.

I stick out my tongue at him.

"Don't worry about it," Liam says, and his hand suddenly lands on my back, applying not one but three pats before he walks up to his brother. "I'll go play with him."

I can still feel the gentle touch of his hand seconds later even though he's probably already forgotten. But I remember. I remember every instant. Every touch. Every smile.

And every amazing moment ruined by Luca De Vos.

Because all I want is his brother.

And all Luca wants is to tease me.

"Jasmine, Jill!"

My mother's voice makes me turn my head.

She's standing in the doorway, glaring us down. "What was all that noise about?"

I swallow. It's not good when my mom looks like that. Like she wants to cut off our heads for ever starting a fight.

"Well, Luca tried to—"

Jasmine elbows me in the side, knocking the wind out of my lungs.

"Luca tried to what?"

"Uh … nothing." I look away. I don't want to get on her bad side.

"We were just playing, that's all," Jasmine fills in.

"Is that true? Luca?" She looks up at him like she expects him to give an honest answer.

"Yes, ma'am," he responds as if he's all nice and stuff, but I see right through that fake act.

I throw him a side-eye, but he ignores me.

I can't bite my tongue. Not on this one. "Luca was teasing me. He stole my crown and said I couldn't be a queen until I married him."

9

My mother begins to frown. Harshly. "*Marry*?!"

Jasmine's lips part. "It was just a game. It didn't mean any—"

Just our mother's raised finger is enough to silence her. "Come inside." She eyes us down. "*All* of you."

Oh boy. I can already feel it coming.

Still, I throw Luca a look. His nostrils flare when he looks at me, but I don't care. He did this.

When we walk in behind her, Luca pushes me forward, and I almost fall into my mother.

"Hey!" I snarl at him.

"What?" He shrugs as we all get inside. "I didn't do anything. Ask Liam. It was him."

"Really, Luca?" Liam slaps his brother on the back of the head, who flinches.

"Mom, Luca—" I begin.

The door slams shut behind us, interrupting my train of thought.

She spins on her heels. The menacing look she throws us could bring even a man as powerful as my father to his knees.

"Jill. How many times have I told you not to fight with boys?"

"But I didn't start—"

"Doesn't matter who started it," she quips, folding her arms. "What matters is that you weren't being nice. And of all the things you could argue about… *marriage*?"

Her eyes have even Liam and Luca silenced. That's how

much of an impact her anger has on us. Because when my mom is angry, there is hell to pay.

"Anne. I think your son should hear this from your mouth," she says, directing her attention toward the couple sitting on the couch. Anne and Lex, Liam and Luca's parents, look at us, and for some reason, I feel like running away.

Anne gets up and walks toward us, folding her arms just like Mom has. And it has the four of us cowering in front of them.

"None of you should be fighting," Anne says. "Or talking about marriage."

"But Luca stole—"

"I don't care what he did, Jill," my mom interjects. "You will not fight with these boys. Is that understood?"

I lower my eyes, but the need to rebel still slips into my voice as I grind my teeth. "Yes, Mom."

"We were just playing around," Luca mutters.

"Luca." His mother throws him a deadly look.

Liam and Jasmine are smart enough to keep their mouths shut. We only seem to make it worse.

"Playing or not … there will be no talk of marriage, understood?" Anne responds.

"Same for you, young ladies," my mom adds, throwing Jasmine and me a look.

I frown. *Why do they care so much?* "Why not?"

"Because the only one who decides who you two will marry …" My father's voice fills the house, bringing goose bumps to my skin, every one of his steps as loud as his voice as he approaches us. "Is me."

My lips part, but I have nothing to say. Not because I don't want to, but because it feels like my voice has been stolen away from me.

I may not be a real princess, but sometimes, I do feel like one.

All locked up in a tower of my parents' making.

And Luca De Vos is waiting for his chance to come and be the cruel prince who rescues me.

Over my dead body.

TWO

LUCA

Age 12

The dead body on the floor doesn't faze me anymore.

I've seen plenty before on our trips downtown when my father's men had to kill someone, and he made my brother and me watch.

The only thing that's got me silent now is the fact that the person holding the gun is my own father.

He always said these were dirty chores best left to our men. But I also know the rules can always be broken, particularly by us.

And especially when it's to save one of our own.

My brother crawls up from the ground, bloodied, wounded. There are cuts all over his back, sharp, like those from a knife. A guard supports him while my dad kills the people in this warehouse one by one until no one is left but us.

When he comes back, he sighs and cleans his gun. The silence is deafening.

"Sorry," my brother says.

Even though he's the one who got hurt.

"Don't ever come out here and try to do my business by yourself again."

"Yes, Dad." Liam can't even look at him.

It's his fault we're here. Dad had to come save him after he tried to run off and prove how strong he is and that he's old enough.

"I get that you want more responsibility, Liam, but now you understand why I'm still the one who runs the show." He tucks his gun away and looks at us. When his hand drops on both my brother's and my shoulder, I'm knocked back into the moment.

"But your enthusiasm doesn't go unnoticed. I'll bring you two along for my daily trips around the city from now on so you can get a feel for how the business is really run." He pats Liam a few times. "You okay, son?"

Liam nods even though I'm sure all those wounds must hurt like hell.

Pain is for the weak. At least, that's what Dad says, and I believe him.

After all, Liam is still alive. These men who tried to hurt him are not.

"Good. We'll get the doc to check you out once we get

home," he says. "Now, hold out your hands. Both of you."

I do what he asks while throwing glances at my brother, wondering what the fuck is going on.

Dad pushes something into our hands. A gold-plated knife with markings on it.

"Keep that on you at all times. Use it when you need to."

I swallow at the thought of slicing through someone the same way they tried to slice through my brother. Not because it scares me … but because it excites me.

And I can't fucking wait to put this thing to good use.

***

Age 14

Another boring day, another boring party somewhere in the middle of nowhere with a bunch of people I don't know and don't want to know either. I grab a stick off the ground and sway it around in the grass, chopping it up while I pretend I'm fighting rivals of our family.

All that yapping at the party distracts me from my game. Ever since we moved to the Netherlands, it's been nothing but business, and I'm bored as hell.

I sigh and shrug it off, waltzing around the grass, trying to find something interesting to poke like a frog. But when I walk around the bush, I find something way more interesting.

Jill Baas is crouched down near a creek outside the premises wearing a really strange fluffy red dress that looks handmade.

What the hell is she doing there?

I quickly make my way there, glancing over my shoulder to ensure no one sees me because our parents told us not to go behind the fenced-off area. But I'm not the only one who never listens to the rules.

As I approach her, I sneak a peek over her shoulder. She's holding something in her hands, but I can't make out what it is.

"What have you got there?"

"Ah!" She shrieks so loudly that she falls down on her butt. "Oh my God, don't scare me like that!"

I snort. "Chicken."

She smashes her fist on my foot, and I jump up and down in pain. "Fuck! Why'd you have to do that?!"

"That's what you get for scaring me," she retorts. "Look at what you did!" She points at something in front of her, something flailing around in the creek.

"What is it?" I ask, getting up close.

"A bunny. It got stuck, and I almost had it pulled out until you scared it away," she hisses at me.

"A bunny?" I say, throwing her a look. "That's why you're behind the fence? Because of some bunny?"

"It's not just a bunny." She gets up and puts her hand against her side. "And it deserves help."

I shrug. "Bunnies can swim."

"Not when their paws might be broken," she spits back. "And if you're not going to help me, back off and leave me alone."

Her sudden spunk shuts me up momentarily as she returns her attention back to the bunny. She reaches for it with her bare hands, but it's out of reach. The bunny is stuck on a branch a little farther up ahead, squealing for help.

I take another glance over my shoulder to make sure no one is looking before I push Jill aside and lean in with my stick, poking the bunny.

"Hey!" Jill yells, trying to push me away too.

Right then, the bunny falls into the water, and I hold the stick in front of the water flow until it stops the bunny.

"Don't hurt it!" Jill tugs at my pants, but I shove her away. "Asshole."

In a quick move, I flick the stick forward to the edge of the creek and lift the bunny from the water. It's soaked and crying, and I hold it close to inspect its paw. There's a wire around its paw that kept it from moving properly, so I rip it off and check the wound. No blood.

"There. It's fine," I say.

When I turn to Jill, her eyes are sparkling, and there's a glossy glow on her face. "Thank you."

I frown. "I didn't do it for you."

She grins and licks her lips as she looks away. "Fine. As long as the bunny is safe."

And somehow, that makes me hate her even more.

Why is she so nice to literally everything and everyone around her?

Why do I even care?

When she tries to grab the bunny, I move away from her.

The look on her face immediately turns sour. "Luca … C'mon. Let me have it."

"No."

She freezes. "I found it first."

I clutch the bunny closer. "And I saved it."

Her nostrils flare, and her eyes almost spew lightning at me. "Luca …" She growls. "Give. Me. The. Bunny."

"No." I pick up the stick and use it as a sword, defending myself. "Finders keepers. It's my bunny now."

Now I've really set her off, and her expression is nothing short of amazing.

She almost explodes. "Luca!"

My mouth bursts into a devious grin. "Come and get it." And I run away as hard as I can with that stupid bunny in my hand, darting through the grass, running on nothing but pure adrenaline.

Because to me, nothing is funnier than pissing off Jill Baas.

And taking whatever happiness she has and making it mine.

***

Jill

Age 18

"You've got the money?" a man in a dirty trench coat mouths to my father.

My mother's hand clenches tightly around mine while she holds Jasmine's in her other as we all watch the men from an appropriate distance. My father wouldn't want us to get too involved yet. It's still his business, after all.

Not any kind of business I'd ever *want* to be involved in, but my mother still forced me to come so I can "learn the ropes." And in this family, choice doesn't exist.

"It's all in here," my father says, as one of our guards hands over the soaked briefcase.

The businessman flicks his fingers, and one of his guards approaches my father to take the case from him. But my eyes can't help skim over the gun hidden underneath his belt buckle. My stomach almost flips over at the sight.

Whatever my father is buying, I don't want to know, and I don't care.

I just want this to be over already.

The guard checks the contents of the briefcase and nods at his superior, who smiles in agreement.

"Our employees will be very happy with this trade," the man says.

Employees from back in the States, no doubt. My father's dirty contacts from when we still lived there.

"Great. I take it the men at The Ruin will accept me as their trading partner?" my father replies.

The guy pulls a cigar from his pocket and throws one at my father, who looks at it like it's the finest cigar he's ever seen. He brings it to his nose and smells it.

"Fuente ..." he murmurs.

"Only the best of the best when you work with The Ruin," the man replies with a wink.

Another guard approaches my father and places a huge box in front of his feet.

"That's only a small fraction."

A guard opens up the box, but I can't see what's inside as it's turned away from us.

"What is it?" Jasmine asks our mother.

"You'll see later," she responds, keeping her eyes on the men, but her nails are digging into my skin as if she's nervous too.

"Happy, Hugo?" the man asks my father.

"More than happy," my father replies as the guard closes the box and two of them haul it to the back of the car.

"I'll let my employees know about our negotiations," the trader replies. "I'm sure they are delighted to have you as a partner."

My father nods. "At least let me offer you a drink before

you're off."

Of course he's trying to make friends with the slime. What a surprise.

The man raises his hand. "As much as I would love to take you up on that offer, we have a flight to catch back to Desolation."

"Desolation?" I whisper. "Where the hell is that?"

"New York," my mother whispers back. "But just watch them, okay?"

"Yeah, yeah." I know she wants me to learn, but I don't think I want to learn any of this.

"Of course, of course," my father says to the man.

"But you will hear from us," the man replies. "Good luck with your endeavors."

"Likewise," my father responds. "Have a great evening, gentlemen."

The men in the coat salute my father, and he turns around and walks back to his black car with dark windows and gets inside, after which his guards finally pull back and hop in too. The car drives off, and I'm left with a nasty feeling deep inside my stomach.

My father rubs his hands together as he comes back toward us. We were huddling in a corner underneath a small ledge of the building. But when my father pulls us in for a big hug, it's almost like we're a normal family.

"Great job, honey," my mother tells him.

He kisses her on the cheeks and me on the forehead.

"Good day today, Vera. A very good day." He puts his

arm through my mother's, and my mother grabs my hand to pull me along. "Let's go to Van Buren's. I'm in the mood for a celebration!"

My ears perk up when he mentions the name of the high-end restaurant in town that we go to every week. "Oh, I love it there."

"You'll do plenty of business there once you're old enough." My father grabs my cheek and squeezes so hard it hurts. He walks back to the car and opens the car door for us. "The De Voses are waiting for us."

Oh … Of course.

Why did I ever think anything other than business would go on in this household?

I sigh out loud, but my father ignores my grumbles as we get in, and the door is closed behind us.

I'm so not looking forward to seeing Luca De Vos again.

Because if there's one thing I'm sure of, it's that an asshole only grows up to be an even bigger asshole.

THREE

Jill

"Hugo!" Lex De Vos exclaims, giving him a pat on the back. "Fijn dat je nog heel bent."

Glad you're still in one piece.

My father laughs as Lex balks, but I don't think it was meant as a joke at all.

"English, guys. Not all of us speak Dutch here," my mother asks with a polite smile, but I can see the annoyance in her eyes.

I'm glad Jasmine and I at least know some Dutch so we can understand what people around us are saying.

"There's no gain if there's no risk," my father tells Lex as he throws off his jacket and hands it to the restaurant manager.

I look around at the beautiful scenery and take in the delicious scents coming from the kitchen. I usually love this restaurant. We come here every week. The Van Buren chain is really one of the best there is when it comes to food. Such a shame it has to be tainted by a certain boy.

"Hello there, Mr. and Mrs. Baas," a guy in a black suit says as he approaches us.

Easton Van Buren. Owner of this restaurant-hotel chain, famous all around the world. And a friend and powerful ally to the Baas family.

"Hello, Easton," my father says. "Hope your best chefs are working tonight."

"Of course," Easton replies. "Only the best for the Baas family." Easton makes a tiny bow. "Let me show you to your table."

"Are you always at this restaurant? I thought you owned multiple," I ask, wondering why we see him every week if he owns that many businesses.

"I do, but I've told my manager to alert me when the Baases make a reservation," he says, winking.

We all follow him to our table.

"We're seated at the back," my father tells Lex. "The VIP suite." A proud smile forms on his face.

"Of course you always get us the finest spot," Lex replies, patting him on the back.

"And my favorite clients deserve only the best," Easton adds, pointing at the table. "There you go."

"Thank you," my mother replies as she looks around at

all the expensive paintings hanging from the wall and touches the fabric of the seats. "Very nice indeed."

But when she steps aside to pull back one of the seats, my eyes find one guy sitting all the way at the back.

Luca.

I swallow.

I haven't seen him for a couple of months now, but every time I do, his wavy dark hair seems to have become even more tousled, his muscles even leaner, and the clothes he wears even more torn. A metal chain wraps around his neck like a stolen souvenir. But one thing has been added to his angsty-boy repertoire: a metal feather dangles from his pierced ear.

I try to look away, but when his dark eyes meet mine, it becomes impossible.

Fuck.

Every damn time I see him, this feeling bubbling underneath the surface of my skin gets worse. An incessant need to hate overcomes me, and my nose twitches as I tear my eyes away from his. Forcing myself to look elsewhere, I find a server pouring some drinks for a couple at a table in the other corner of the room. It's not at all interesting, but I had to do something to stop myself from looking at him.

Even now, I can still feel his eyes boring into my chest.

I can't fucking wait until this obligatory dinner party is over.

"Jill?" My mother commands my attention. "Are you going to sit?"

Everyone's eyes are on me right now, but only one gaze draws out my ire.

I look around to find my seat, but I can feel the blood draining from my face.

Liam, who has beefed up a significant amount since I last saw him, is sitting at the closest corner, and Jasmine has parked herself on the seat right next to him.

Which means … the only chair left is situated right next to Luca.

The smug grin growing on his face as he watches me lose my shit is making me want to turn around and march right out of here.

"Jill. We'd like to have dinner. *Nu.*" My father's stern look reminds me why I can't ever deny him.

I don't speak Dutch that fluently yet, but I know that word. *Nu.* Now. He only uses his mother tongue when he wants to be stern, but he's been using it more and more since we've moved here.

I sigh out loud and collect myself before walking over to Luca's side of the table. His eyes are on me at all times, the glint inside them taunting me. He enjoys this. I just know he does.

Fucker.

I grab the seat and pull back, the wooden legs scraping against the floor. Liam finally looks up too, and when I plop down on my seat, even Jasmine throws me a glare.

"Jill," she whispers, "We're trying to talk."

"I'm not stopping you," I reply as I scoot my chair

closer to the table but as far away from Luca as possible.

"You're not stopping *anyone.*"

I freeze in my chair at the sound of his voice so close to my ear that I can feel it reverberate through my entire body.

When I turn my head, he's right there, invading my space like he enjoys getting me all worked up.

My nostrils flare, and I look away again, determined not to let him ruin this dinner. Especially because it's important to my parents.

"Hi to you too, Luca," I reply, putting down my clutch bag. "Happy to see you too."

"I never said I was *happy* to see you," he retorts, moving away again to cook in his own juice.

I roll my eyes. "Same. I lied." I grab a handful of peanuts and shove them in my mouth before I say something I'll regret.

A server places drinks on the table even though I didn't order anything. I guess my father did it for us. Typical. Always in control.

"Don't you know it's not nice to lie?" Luca retorts, planting his hand underneath his head to look at me from an angle. "Do you ever say what you really think, Jill?"

I shrug, chewing on my peanuts. "I'm a mystery."

"A mystery I'd like to unravel." The smirk that forms on his face makes me swallow, and I almost choke on some of the peanuts.

"Right," I mutter, wiping the salt off my hands. "Hey, when is dinner coming?" I ask my mother from across the table.

"We haven't ordered yet, darling," she responds. "But they'll come and take our order soon, so just relax and have some fun with the boys, okay?"

Before I can open my mouth, she's already turned her head back to Luca's mother, Anna.

Damn.

I turn my head toward Liam, but he seems occupied with Jasmine. Both of their faces adorn smiles that just scream awkward, but I don't know if it's because of this dinner or because of the conversation they had.

"Hey," Luca whispers in my ear. "The server's over there. Maybe he'll come over if you ... beg."

I close my eyes, trying to get rid of the fire raging in my throat before I snap and let it all out.

He's just trying to mess with you, Jill.

Ignore him.

"So, Liam," I say, butting in to Jasmine's conversation. "How is your school? Do you like it there?"

"Uh ..." He crosses looks back and forth between Jasmine and me.

I hope she doesn't mind. I understand why she wanted to sit next to him, though. He's gotten even more handsome than I remember. Like the younger version of Heath Ledger.

When his mouth opens, we're all hanging on his words. "It's fine, I just—"

"He's lying. He hates the school," Luca interjects, leaning in a little too close.

"Really?" Jasmine frowns. "Is that true?"

"No," Liam responds, throwing Luca an angry look.

Luca shrugs. "Fine then, lie. I won't lie. I hate it there."

"You, *not* enjoying school?" I raise a brow. "I'm shocked."

My turn to toy with him.

He throws me a short, smug, and totally rude smile. "Not all of us are a Goody Two-shoes."

My lips part, and my brows furrow in disgust. "Being good at studying is not an insult, you dickhead."

"It is when you're more buried in books than people. Boys. Girls. It doesn't matter to me." His eyebrow flicks up, and the second it registers with me what he just said, a wicked smile forms on his face like he can see straight into my mind.

Fuck. Him.

"Oh my God," Jasmine scoffs, laughing it off. "Awkward."

"*Ooookay*," Liam says, tapping the table with his fingers.

It's quiet for a moment. Too quiet. And it makes me grab more peanuts and shove them in my mouth. Even if Luca is staring me down, I won't be browbeat by him.

I listen in to some of the conversations our parents are having, but I only catch a few phrases about some kind of "cargo" and that they'll be happy to "distribute" it to their dealers.

Not that I want to know. It's all shady as hell, and we all know, but no one cares, and neither do I. As my father says, he earns the hard money to pay for our futures, so I can't complain.

"Well, anyway, we're switching schools soon," Jasmine says, trying to change the subject.

"Really? Which one?" Liam asks.

"Ours."

Luca's voice overarches our entire corner of the table, and the silence that follows makes all the hairs on the back of my neck stand up.

Jasmine turns her head to him, and Liam follows, forcing me to remove my elbow.

"Wait, what?" Jasmine says, looking confused. "Did you say *ours?*"

Luca's tongue dips out to wet his lips, and when he parts them, he doesn't look at her ... he looks solely at me.

"I asked your parents, and it's true ... you're joining us in class."

My eyes and mouth widen, but I can't say a word even though I try my best.

I didn't know.

I didn't know the school our parents had chosen was the one *they* go to.

How could they not tell *me* but tell *him?*

And why did I fail to ask?

Dammit.

No one says a word, not even Liam, even though I'm begging in my head for him to deny it.

But he doesn't.

Suddenly, my father gets up from his seat with a champagne glass in his hand and clears his throat. "I'd like to say a toast. To our partners. Our friends. Our sons and daughters." He looks at us. "To our future."

Why is he looking at us like that?

"Cheers!"

Our parents raise their glasses, and they all look at us like they're waiting for us to join. So I pick up the glass and lift it without breaking a smile. I don't know what exactly we're toasting to, and I doubt my parents will ever tell me.

But from the vicious smirk on Luca's face, I know he's not toasting to any of the business deals our parents are concocting with that precious cargo my father bought.

"To many more years," Luca adds, and then he turns his head to me in spite, winking.

He's celebrating the fact that we're switching schools … and that he's going to turn my life into a living hell.

FOUR

LUCA

Hours later

There is only one thing I hate more than being left alone to my own damn thoughts, and that's being left alone with the most impossible girl on the planet.

Jill Baas.

She stares at me from across the black velvet couch, still wearing that gold-flaked beige dress she wore at the restaurant that looks handmade, but it's much more sophisticated than that red dress I saw her in years ago.

She clutches her panty-clad knees like she's afraid they might melt off from the fire crackling in the fireplace. But it isn't the fire she should be afraid of.

"Nice dress," I say.

"Thanks," she replies, getting all flustered. "Made it

32

myself."

"I can see that."

The blush immediately disappears, and she looks stoically ahead like she's trying to vanish into the couch from embarrassment.

It wasn't meant as an insult.

Though I guess she'd take it that way.

I part my legs farther and shift in my seat, trying to get comfortable while wasting my time, but it's clearly not working as I'm getting more agitated by the second. Maybe, just maybe, it doesn't fucking help that this girl can't stop looking at me like a lost sheep.

"What?" I bark.

She shrugs, still obviously on edge. "Nothing."

I sigh and fish a smoke from my pocket, throwing the package her way. "Here. Have a smoke. Maybe it'll calm you down."

"I'm calm, thanks," she replies, not even looking in the direction of the package like she's afraid it could give her cancer on sight.

I shake my head and light my cig. "Suit yourself."

Shit, I've never had this hard of a time entertaining 'guests' my father brings home, but I guess there's a first time for everything.

With Jill, I never know what to expect. If anything at all.

Taunting her is only fun if she reacts, but all she's done is deny me and it pisses me off.

"Where are Liam and Jasmine?" she asks.

Of course, she's more interested in them.

I take a drag of my cig, watching the panic settle in her eyes when she realizes she might have to spend all her time with me alone. "I don't know."

"Maybe we should go upstairs and look for them."

She's that desperate for him?

A smoldering fire begins deep inside me, but I ignore it. Maybe I should poke the dragon a little, see what happens.

I blow out the smoke. "And interrupt their fuck session?"

Her eyes widen and her whole body tenses up.

Shit, I'd almost say like it matters a little too much to her.

"Relax, he won't hurt her," I add.

She gets up and starts walking to the door, so I jump up and catch up with her, blocking the door just in time. "Whoa, whoa, where are you going?"

She stares me down like she's mad I stopped her. "Upstairs."

"Why?" I raise a brow.

"Because … you're boring." She folds her arms like she means business.

Me, boring? I think the fuck not.

She's just trying to get away from me … and run into Liam's arms.

Pathetic.

"You wanted to see if they're really fucking or not," I say.

She cocks her head. "Or maybe you just don't want to face the fact that you're a horrible host." She tries to pass me, but I shut the door. "What's your problem?"

"You," I say, eyeing her up and down until she backs off a little. "And I don't intend to let that slide."

She rolls her eyes and marches back to the couch. "Fine. Have it your way. We can sit here all night and talk about nothing and do nothing. Happy now?"

"Never," I respond as I come to join her. But when I sit down beside her, she scoots over to get farther away from me. "You scared of me, bunny?"

"Bunny?" she scoffs, and it takes a while for her brain to register why I called her that.

She shakes her head. "Do *not* call me that."

"Skittish little bunny you are." I lick my lips at the sight of her red-hot face. I love the way she looks at me, like she could bite my head off and fuck me over at the same time. "You gonna jump in some water too?"

"Oh fuck you, I haven't forgiven you for that," she growls back, but it only makes me laugh.

"Good. Stay mad," I respond.

"What happened to that bunny anyway?" she asks, curious as ever.

I raise a brow and lick my lips. "You'd like to know, wouldn't you?"

When I wink, she rolls her eyes. "Ugh. Typical."

I don't know why I enjoy seeing her ticked off so much, but I do.

Maybe it's because she's always pretending to be so perfect. Like she's on a pedestal that I can't ever reach.

I take another whiff of my smoke. Damn these thoughts. I need something stronger. This smoke isn't taking the edge off.

I pull out my phone and text someone.

"What are you doing?" Jill asks.

I put my smoke down on the ashtray on the table. "Nothing."

I finish the text and send it off. But when I look up to see that grumbling face of hers, I almost want to burst into laughter.

"Oh, c'mon. You've gotta give me something," she says.

"Or what?" I raise my brow. "Afraid you might … miss out?"

Her lip twitches as she snarls, "You wish."

A smirk forms on my lips. "Maybe."

She grabs the pillow lying next to her and chucks it at my face. The victorious grin that appears on her face makes me pause. Did she do this to hurt me, or is she trying to deflate the tension?

I throw it back, but she's not prepared, and the rage that appears on her face is magnificent to see. She chucks it right back at me, and it lands much harder than before. Obviously, I have to respond by throwing it back with equal strength.

We keep throwing it back and forth until we're both grinning and standing up while throwing pillows at each other. It's going down hard, but I'm not giving up even though she throws that pillow using her full body weight.

She puts so much effort in the last one that she loses her balance and topples over … right on top of me.

We both fall onto the couch with only a pillow separating us, and I stare into the most beautiful, piercing blue eyes I've ever seen.

The silence is deafening, but it doesn't compare to the overwhelming feeling of her body on top of mine. Of all the curves of her body pressing against me, her legs splayed against mine, and the fog of her breath mingling with mine.

One. Two. Three seconds pass before her pretty face turns red.

Suddenly, the door behind us opens.

Looking up, she scrambles to her feet, breaking the connection. And I'm left with the biggest hard-on I've ever felt in my entire fucking life.

Fuck.

She pulls at her dress which has crept up a little, and my cock twitches in response.

"Well … guess you two are having fun," Jasmine says as she walks in with Liam following suit.

"I just fell, that's all," Jill explains, clearing her throat. "What were you guys doing?"

"Oh, just talking," Liam answers, scratching the back of his head. "But I got hungry, so I'm making a sandwich. Y'all want some?"

"No, thanks," we all say in sync.

He shrugs. "Suit yourself." And he marches into the kitchen.

"What kind of stuff did you talk about?" Jill asks as Jasmine walks toward the couch.

"Oh, nothing serious. School. Our parents. You know."

"So nothing … happened?" Jill mutters.

I snort, but the two girls ignore me. Of course she'd ask that.

Jasmine looks confused. "No …? Should something have happened?"

Jill visibly relaxes, a sigh lifting her shoulders up and down.

Fuck. I really wish I hadn't noticed.

I don't want to listen to any of this.

"Whatever," I say, and I get up.

The doorbell rings.

Fucking finally.

I immediately march toward it.

"Expecting someone?" Jasmine says.

I just open the front door and let in the girl with the long, flowing blond hair and giant tits that I can't wait to bury my face in. But the second I close the front door, my eyes land on Jill and her horrified face, and it puts a damper on my horny mood.

"Is that the girl you texted?" Jill asks.

"Yeah, so?" I reply, taking the girl's coat. I grab her hand and drag her with me. "C'mon, Gillian. Let's go."

"What?" Jill frowns as I pull her toward the stairs. "I

thought you were supposed to—"

"You have Jasmine now. Entertain yourself," I retort.

"You know what our parents—"

"I don't care," I interject, barking a little too harshly, which makes her sink into her seat. Still, I can't get over the sour look on her face, and it pisses me off even more.

"You want to come lie in my bed too?" I ask, letting my tongue run along my lips.

Her eyes widen, and her eyes twitch as she tries to hide her shame. "No, no, no. No, thank you."

I wink. "Suit yourself." And I head upstairs with this giggling girl who I'll use to fuck my anger away.

And then I'll finish my smoke.

FIVE

Jill

"Oh, my God. Can you believe that?" Jasmine asks.

I don't even know how to answer. I'm that stunned.

Did Luca seriously just bring a girl in to … have sex with her?

My skin crawls, and my stomach contorts, but I ignore the sting.

"Is he going to do what I think he's going to do?" Jasmine sits down on the couch opposite of me.

I nod a few times, rubbing my lips. "Yep."

A part of me cannot fucking wait until this night is over. But another part of me wants to go upstairs and tear that girl away from him so I can slap the ever-living shit out of him.

"Damn, what an ass," Jasmine says, and she looks at his smoke. "Yuck." She puts it out into the tray so it no longer

40

smells. "You okay?"

I nod again. "I'm fine. I'm just … bored out of my mind and can't wait to get out of here."

"Same, girl," she says, rubbing her legs. "Even that talk with Liam."

"What?"

Liam? Boring? I can't fathom those two words belonging in the same sentence.

"Yeah, I just can't connect with him, but Mom said I should try, so I did." She sighs. "But all he wants to do is talk about sports and school." She rolls her eyes.

"What did you expect?" I raise a brow.

She snorts. "Well, I don't know. Deeper stuff." She grabs a pillow and clutches it to her stomach. "What did you talk about with Luca?"

The second she mentions his name, the image of me lying on top of him flashes through my mind and makes my cheeks hot again. I can still see those dark eyes in front of me, still feel his breath on my lips, and the thought alone makes goose bumps scatter on my skin.

Nope, nope, nope.

"Nothing," I deadpan.

She snorts again. "Nothing? C'mon, there must be something interesting. These boys can't both be boring."

"They're not," I say, maybe a little too fast. "At least, Liam isn't. But no one likes to be set up by their parents."

"You're right. Maybe I'll go check and see what they're up to."

She gets up and throws the pillow back on the couch, walking to the office where our parents are having a very important business conversation.

"Are you sure that's a good idea?" I ask. "Mom said we weren't allowed to go inside."

"They want us to take over someday, don't they? Shouldn't we also get to know their business?"

Well, she has a point there, I guess. Besides, it's not like I can stop her. Once Jasmine has made up her mind, that's that.

She opens the door and peeks inside. A smile appears on her face. I hear some voices but can't tell what they're saying. She steps inside, her body disappearing behind the door, which clicks into place.

Great. More silence.

Liam suddenly comes back from the kitchen with three glasses of Coke fizzing away. And the smile is right back on my face again as he places one of the glasses on the table in front of me.

"There you go."

I'm surprised he didn't ask their butler to do it for him. I know they have plenty of people working for them. But I guess he enjoys pretending not to be rich.

"Thanks," I say.

"I know you didn't ask, but I figured you might've been thirsty too."

He's always so thoughtful and considerate of others. Unlike Luca, who is driven only by his own egotistical desires.

"Where'd Jasmine run off to?" he asks as he places the last Coke down and sits on the couch next to me.

"She's in 'the room.'" I make quotation marks with my fingers.

He frowns. "Never pegged her to be that interested in the business side of things."

I shrug and pick up my Coke to take a sip. "I'm not either, but I guess we gotta learn someday anyway. Might as well make it today."

Liam gulps down some of his Coke. "I don't know. To be honest, I don't care all that much about the business side of things even though I'm the first in line. But the thought of having to take over all that fucked-up stuff makes me feel dead inside." He shakes it off like bugs crawl over his skin.

"I get it. I feel the same way," I say, finally feeling like I have a connection with him. "Our parents are always forcing us to go everywhere without ever asking us what we want."

"Yeah, exactly," he responds, which makes me smile. "And it's messed up they're dealing weapons and drugs."

I never heard it said out loud before like that, but we all know what our parents do behind closed doors.

"I know it's what they do to make a living, and I'm grateful for all the opportunities and the stuff they've given me." He looks around at all the luxury, the expensive furniture, even his clothes. "But to be honest … all that fucked-up shit they do makes me want to run far away."

"I totally understand," I say, tucking my hair behind my

ear. "I feel the same pressure from my parents to always appear perfect and to fall in line. Like this business is the only thing that matters, and that we're supposed to take over, and that there's no way out."

He nods a few times before grabbing his Coke. "See, this is exactly what I tried to talk to Jasmine about, but she doesn't get it. She thinks it's an honor to be part of the family business." He sighs and looks away for a second. "I wish I could see it her way. I know it would make her happy."

Make ... her ... happy.

A chill runs up and down my spine.

"I like seeing her smile."

His words are like a knife straight to the heart.

Suddenly, the door opens up again, and I look up, only to be horrified by Luca kissing that same girl on the cheeks. But not just that ... her shirt is on the wrong way, which means that it was completely off at one point.

Fuck.

I clench the glass of Coke so hard it might break, so I quickly put it down.

"Had fun up there?" I ask as he helps the girl put on her coat, after which she leaves through the front door again. "That was quick."

With an arrogant smirk on his face, he strides over to me, sliding behind the couch to whisper in my ear, "You just wish I took you up there ..."

A moan follows at the end of his sentence.

All the hairs on my body stand up as I clench my legs together to prevent whatever I felt from rushing down between my thighs.

He's just playing with me, trying to get me to go off like a damn bomb. I won't grant him that kind of fun.

"Fuck you," I retort, and I grab the pillow again and smack it right into his face.

He throws the pillow far away. "Aw, bunny got all flustered." Then he jumps over the couch and plops down on his butt right beside me. Dammit.

"So what are you two doing?" Luca asks, looking at his brother. "Weren't you having fun with Jasmine?"

"We were just talking, that's all," Liam responds, eyeing him up and down while gulping down the rest of his Coke. "Unlike you."

"Hey, I don't tell you what to do in your room either," Luca retorts, plastering both his arms on the back of the couch to claim ownership. A show of dominance. But the thought of his hands so close to my face makes my body zing in ways I did not expect.

"But I guess you're just jealous," Luca adds.

His brother makes a *pfft* sound. "You wish."

"A trio?" Luca raises his brow. "Thought you'd never ask."

My jaw drops, and I throw a punch, which misses him. "Luca! He's your brother!"

"What? It's not like our dicks would touch," he scoffs. "But if we both take a different side—"

45

"That's enough," Liam interjects.

"What?" Luca responds, still egging us on. "We're always together anyway while our parents do shady business in a dark room. Might as well have fun while waiting."

I don't know if he's joking or if he's serious.

I turn to face him. "Have you always been this obsessed with sex?"

His tongue darts out to wet his lips in such a sexual way that I can't stop focusing on it, and I hate it. "Depends with who."

Oh, God.

"So that's why you invited that girl ... Could've just bought a blow-up doll," Liam taunts.

Luca throws him a glare. "There's nothing in this world more important than sex, money, and power."

Liam shifts in his seat. "Happiness."

What a breath of fresh air.

Until Luca shifts forward too, his hand on his knee, his eyes spitting fire, and it suddenly feels like all the air has been sucked out of this room.

"Fuck happiness," Luca spits.

"That's the only thing you can't buy," Liam adds. "Maybe that's why you've never felt it."

Luca shoots up from the couch and stomps over to his brother, who also gets up from the couch as they face off. "Shut the fuck up."

Wow. So unnecessary.

"Why? Because I exposed a part of you that you don't

want other people to see?" Liam says, raising a brow. "Especially *her*?"

Liam throws me a single glance, but it's enough to make me sit up straight and feel like the spotlight is on me.

Why is this about me all of a sudden?

"Whoa," I mutter. "I have nothing to do with your fighting and—"

Luca shoves Liam, interrupting me. "I told you to shut the fuck up."

"Okay, I'm out of here," I say before they can pin this on me. I quickly get up from the couch and walk to the back door leading out to the yard, shutting the door behind me before they can protest. I'm gonna go for a walk outside in the garden and take a breather.

Because my mind cannot wrap around what just happened in there.

It was almost like … Liam tried to say that Luca was hiding something from me.

And that it involves happiness.

I close my eyes and sigh.

It doesn't make any sense.

Maybe it's just boys being boys. And I don't want any part in that.

***

LUCA

"Great. Look what you did," I spit at Liam. "You chased her away."

"Don't try to pin this on me, dude. You're the one who brought a whore into the house."

"I can do whatever the fuck I want with my life, and that girl was no whore."

"Sure you can," Liam scoffs. "But we all see through your lies. I know what you're doing."

I frown. "Tell me what I'm doing then." I fold my arms. "Tell me then if you know me as well as you think you do."

"Like I'd make it so easy for you to hit me," Liam scoffs. "Pass."

"Like you're so perfect," I retort, throwing a glance at the door where our parents are scheming. I know Jasmine's in there. She's the only one of us actually interested in their business. "You're trying to get the only girl who doesn't even want you."

Liam shoves me so hard I almost fall back onto the couch. "Don't you talk about Jasmine like that!"

"Relax, bro. It doesn't even fucking matter. That's what I've been trying to tell you all along. We don't make the decisions. *They* do," I say, grabbing the only leftover Coke to throw it back in one go. I plant the glass back down on the table firmly and focus my attention on him. "So go and bang someone. Anyone. Get it out of your system." I point a finger at his chest. "But you're a hypocrite if you think I'm the only one."

"You only care about sex, right?" He grabs my finger. "Keep lying to yourself. Maybe you'll convince someone."

"I don't need to tell you what I care about," I hiss.

"But do you care about *her*?"

My nostrils flare. I'm about this close to punching out his two front teeth.

But the punishment that would follow when our parents find out isn't worth it.

"If you do … stay the fuck away." He taps my chest now. "She doesn't want you."

"Fuck you," I say, and I turn around.

"Don't be so fucking afraid of the truth, Luca," Liam shouts as I walk off.

I throw him the finger without even looking at him. "Look in the mirror, dick."

I walk out the door and slam it shut behind me. I don't need to listen to Liam. He knows as well as I do that I'm not the only one running from his problems. He thinks he's perfect, but he's not. Unfortunately, our parents don't see him the way I do, and it pisses me off.

Always the prodigy, the one to rule the empire.

Fuck him.

If I can't have what I want … I'll take everything else this world has to offer.

SIX

LUCA

Weeks later

The cigarette in my mouth can't burn enough to light a spark inside me. I feel cold. Hard like the stone fence I'm sitting on, gazing at the students passing by as they enter the school.

Until finally, a car parks in front of the gates. And not just any car. The armored black limo with darkened windows is over the top, just like the family who owns it.

I snort and shake my head, stubbing out the bud of my cigarette on the fence. But when I look up again, the sight of the girl stepping out of the car, clutching her bag while brushing aside a few strands of her long luscious locks in the wind, warms that dead heart inside my body.

It's amazing how she stands tall and proud, facing the

crowd in front of her despite knowing exactly how they feel about people like us, people involved in the criminal world.

I knew the second I stepped onto the grounds of this expensive school, people would hate my guts. I didn't make any apologies and didn't care in the slightest how they would react. I'm used to it. I know where I belong in society, and it's at the bottom. I'm one of those rich assholes whose parents control an empire with vast influence across the country. It isn't ruled by the political parties … it's ruled by us.

And that creates envy.

Hatred.

The kind that makes you want to lash out. But I've turned it into a badge I wear with pride.

If only she'd see it that way.

That girl with the pretty blond hair, wearing those high heels and red lips like she doesn't care or fear anything.

That girl with her fake innocence and fake confidence … *That* girl is a fucking liar.

I try to look away, but every single time I look at other girls, she still captures my attention, like a moth finding the flame, and it makes me sick to my stomach.

She's everything I shouldn't ever want, everything I couldn't ever have.

She's … *everything.*

Everything bad.

Wrong.

Dirty.

Enticing.

Like a piece of candy waiting to be unwrapped.

And I fucking hate that part about myself.

That part that wants.

Needs.

Craves.

That girl isn't and won't ever be mine.

Jill.

***

Jill

When the armored limo finally arrives at school, I clutch my bag close to my chest and say a little prayer. I'm not normally this anxious, but the fact Jasmine and I are arriving in a limo will surely turn some heads. I didn't want to do it, but our parents gave us no choice.

I look up at the giant gates and the building behind it. *Kaspar Gymnasium.* English High School in the Netherlands for the rich and famous. This school houses all the elite students from abroad. The ones who don't speak Dutch but whose parents still work here. All rich kids who don't want to be here, just like us.

Lucky for me, I only have to be here one more year until

I graduate.

I don't understand why we had to switch schools this late, though.

But I can make a guess.

We quickly jump out and say goodbye to the driver, who will pick us up again once school is over. Walking off the premises isn't allowed for the time being, according to my father. A peril of doing the business he's in.

Jasmine and I try to blend in with the crowd, but it's hard when everybody's looking at us like we're trying to make ourselves look more important than we are. Some throw us smiles like they're trying to impress us, but others only sneer at us, and it makes me want to snarl at them.

Someone laughs at me.

I know it's not just because of who I am or the family I belong to, but also because of how I dress. Sometimes, I make my own clothes, and today, I decided to wear one such outfit to my first day at school.

"Ridiculous," someone mutters as they walk past me.

Maybe it was a bad idea.

Jasmine throws the person an evil glare.

"Just ignore them," she tells me. "They don't have style anyway," she adds, sliding on her sunglasses.

My hand firmly clutches her arm. I'm so glad she always has my back.

I don't like it when people laugh at me for my creations. It's just something I like to do in my spare time. A little rebellion against my parents' brutal reign.

"What's your first class again?" Jasmine asks while on the way inside.

"Oh … lemme check." I completely forgot after getting out of the car and being stared down by other kids. I fetch my schedule from my bag. "Economy."

"Mine's Dutch, so I guess we'll see each other at break time," Jasmine responds.

We give each other a short hug before she walks in the opposite direction, and I'm left clutching my bag, feeling lost in the masses. Everyone stares me up and down like I've got shit stuck to my face, but I know that's not the case. I simply can't rinse away the stench of criminals—aka my family.

I close my eyes for a second and take a breath.

Just get through the day, no matter how badly you want to run.

This is your life. This is your future.

The future your parents gave you.

Plenty of people would kill to have this life.

Opening my eyes, I plaster on a smile, then look at the time on my phone.

Suddenly, someone bumps into me, knocking my schedule and phone from my hand.

People scurry past me, but I have no clue what's going on. I pick up my phone and schedule, but I notice a fight up ahead when I look up.

Fuck, I really shouldn't be interested. Class could start at any moment now … but I can't help myself and still walk toward it. I tuck my phone in my pocket and my schedule in my bag, but the second I realize who's fighting, I drop my bag.

"Jasmine!" I scream, pushing through the crowd to get to her.

A boy pulls at her hair while another tries to steal her bag away from her.

"That's what you get for shoving me!" one of them shouts.

"Fuck you for calling my sister a clown!" she yells back.

A clown?

Me?

My eyes flash down to my outfit for just a second. All I see is the yellow plaid skirt I sewed and the red top I'm wearing, wondering what part of this makes me look like a clown.

A sudden punch being thrown pulls me out of my thoughts.

Jasmine doesn't back down and defends herself with everything she's got, despite being bullied by three boys from all sides. But one of them tackles her from behind, and she lands on the floor with an *oompf.*

I jump into the fray, not giving a shit about the repercussions as I smack one of the boys right on the head.

The other two start to circle around us while I stand over Jasmine to protect her.

"C'mon then!" I yell at them, holding my fists up.

When one of them approaches me, I swiftly throw a punch, knocking out a tooth.

Another guy grabs me from behind and puts me in an elbow lock. I gasp, but the air gets trapped in my throat.

"Get off her!" Jasmine yells from beneath me as she tries to get up, but another one of the boys keeps her on the floor with his boot pressed firmly on her chest.

"You two don't even fucking belong here," the one boy I hit says.

I spit in his face. His face turns red with rage.

He slaps me in the face so hard my head turns.

And my eyes connect with the only boy I hoped wouldn't see me in this position.

Luca De Vos.

But his eyes don't show that familiar spark or that devilish smirk on his upturned lips.

Instead, all they show is the craving for violence.

***

LUCA

The second my eyes find hers as she stands in the middle of a crowd, throwing fisticuffs with a bunch of guys, I stop and drop everything I was holding. I rush to the scene, ignoring people around me shouting at me, pushing past them to land straight into the fight.

And before the guy can punch her again for daring to spit on him, I throw him an uppercut to the chest. He heaves and bends over from the pain, saliva dribbling onto the floor.

"What the fuck, man!?" the guy splutters.

He quickly rises and throws me a punch. I can't dodge in time, taking it to the face, but I don't flinch.

Suddenly, some arms fling around my neck and pull me into a headlock. The other guy takes the opportunity to give me back the same uppercut, and I groan with pain.

"Luca!" Jill screams, and she tries to punch the guy's back.

He merely swipes at her with one hand, throwing her to the hard stone floor.

Rage bursts through my veins, and I roar as I tear away from the arms behind me. I swiftly kick the guy in front of me and punch him in the face. I spin on my heels to jam my knee into the other guy's balls.

He yowls in pain and falls down, clutching his junk. "Why the fuck are you butting in?"

The second I pull out my knife, all of them back away.

"Don't you dare fucking lay another hand on her," I say through gritted teeth, and I throw a snarl at the one guy left standing, but he quickly backs away with his hands raised like a dog with his tail between his legs.

"What? Scared of a little knife?" I say, flicking it around to make their eyes follow the blade.

Jill is beside her sister, helping her get up, while I stare at the crowd surrounding us to make sure none of them gets any ideas.

"What is going on here?"

Everyone suddenly starts to scramble as Dean Hans barges into the hallway. I quickly tuck my knife back into my pocket and pretend nothing happened.

Hans stops in his tracks the second he spots us, his eyes taking in the bruises on Jill's face, the mess of Jasmine's backpack scattered all over the floor, and my thick lip and bloody gashes. Dean Hans's face darkens as he marches toward us and grabs me by the collar.

"De Vos, alweer?!" *Again.* "How many times do I have to tell you to stop fighting with other students?"

"He wasn't." Jill suddenly speaks up, taking a step forward. Her hand briefly touches my arm, and a jolt of lightning shoots up my veins I can only describe as powerful. Addictive.

"He was protecting us."

The dean looks at both of us to try to discern the truth from our eyes, but I don't have any lies to give him. Not today.

He sucks in a breath and barks, "Into my office. All of you." When he marches away, he throws us all a glance over his shoulder. "Now."

***

When the dean's done berating us, I head straight back through that same hallway and keep my head low. I'm already glad I wasn't expelled for fighting. At least those assholes will get punished too, but Dad will be pissed if I keep drawing attention to myself like that.

Suddenly, someone tugs at my arm, so I turn. It's none other than Jill, staring at me with this sickly sweet smile on her face, which makes me want to scream.

"Hey," she says as Jasmine walks past us and waves. "I just wanted to thank you." Jill's cheeks turn faintly red, almost the same color as that red top of hers, and for some reason, my eyes are immediately drawn down toward those tits hiding underneath and—

Fuck, don't go there.

So I look back up at her face, but I don't know whether to walk away or to stay and stare at her and those pink cheeks, those blue eyes, those luscious red lips that make me want to—

This isn't any better. At all.

Fuck.

She brings a tissue up to my face, gently blotting at my busted lip. "Sorry about that. I didn't want you to get hurt."

She … didn't want *me* to get hurt?

Without thinking, I grab her wrist. "Don't."

"What? I'm just trying to help," she replies.

I drag her closer by her wrist. "I didn't ask for your help." I shove her hand away. "And I don't need your thanks either."

"Well, I'm sorry for appreciating your help," she scoffs, her face turning sour. "So much for saving us."

When no one is watching, I push her up against the wall,

planting a hand beside her face. "I don't save people. I hurt people." I fish the knife from my pocket and show it to her. "You think I took that beating to save you? Wrong."

"Then why? Why go through the effort."

I lean in, smelling the scent of fear on her breath as I go in closer and closer and closer until I'm right beside her ear, and I whisper, "Because I crave violence."

It's in my blood. My very essence.

Pain. Blood. Murder.

It's what we've been taught by my parents early on in life.

What we've been told is the only means to get what you want.

Power.

And with power ... you control the world.

I lean away again, tucking the knife back into my pocket. "Don't say thank you to a monster. You'll regret it one day."

And I take my hand off the wall and walk off, determined not to look back for fear of what I might do.

What I might *want*, more than power, more than anything else in this entire fucking world.

What I might *take* if she starts being nice to me.

Her.

SEVEN

LUCA

WHACK!

The strike of his hand against my face hits harder than any punch I've received from the fuckers I destroyed at school or wherever else.

"That's for fighting at school," my father says.

Another strike to the other side of my face makes my lip twitch in resentment.

But it's nothing compared to the pain I've felt numerous times before … and not just by my father's hand.

"You should know better than to draw attention to yourself and tarnish our family's name."

I didn't even get a chance to explain that I was trying to …

Save Jill and Jasmine.

No, fuck that. I'm no knight in shining armor.

And my father probably wouldn't even care.

He slaps me twice more just because he enjoys seeing the blood rush to my skin. I got my wicked cravings from somewhere, and it wasn't my mother whose genes passed it on.

"And that's for bringing girls into my fucking house," my father seethes.

I don't know how he found out.

Probably the cameras.

I should've covered them.

"How dare you? How fucking dare you disobey me?" he says, his voice filled with contempt. "I told you, you and your brother need to start taking your lives seriously."

I don't respond. Nothing I can say will make his rage go away. Mine never does. And I didn't get it from a stranger.

"You're a disgrace," he says, and he spits on the floor in front of my feet. "Don't ever fucking humiliate me again, Luca, or there will be hell to pay." He points at the door. "Go to your room."

He doesn't have to say it twice. I'm already out the door.

Fuck him and fuck that high horse he rode in on.

I can do whatever the fuck I want. No one's gonna stop me, not even his harsh rules or the hard hand he hits with.

It's not the first time I got hurt, and it definitely won't be the last.

I learned a long time ago my father uses violence to get what he wants, whether it's with his competitors ... or his own damn son.

Nothing is forbidden. Violence is normal when you're a part of the mafia.

Mafia.

That one word we're not allowed to use. As if denying its existence makes it easier to swallow what my family really is.

A bunch of mobsters who use violence to get rich and powerful. And to force their own damn family into the same fucking life, even if they end up hating you for it.

Fuck this.

I hurry up the stairs and stomp into my room, slamming the door shut ... only to find Liam sitting on my fucking bed.

"Get out," I bark.

"No, c'mon," he says, leisurely lounging on his elbows. "I'm your brother. Let's talk."

"No," I spit back, my palms turning into fists.

"You've made enough enemies," Liam says. "Don't turn me into one too."

"What the fuck do you want?"

He sits up straight. "I just wanna know what happened."

"I got in a fight at school. Big deal," I reply.

"I thought you said you were done with that?" he says.

I cock my head. "Yeah, well, that was before those two Baas girls tried to walk all over the school grounds in those fucking glass slippers, wearing that red lipstick like they owned the fucking place."

My brother's brows rise in that annoying way they always do when his interest is piqued. "Sounds to me like you paid a little too much attention to them."

"No fucking shit," I respond. "It's kinda hard not to notice when they're making new '*friends.*'" I make quotation marks with my fingers.

"So you got into a fight for *them*?"

I pause. I almost want to say it out loud.

Not for them. For her.

But I don't.

"They were being mobbed by three guys. What else was I supposed to do?" I yell. "It's not like I had a choice."

"You could've walked away," Liam says.

"Oh, like you would have," I scoff. "While your precious Jasmine is on the floor, begging for you to save her."

"Hey, don't make this about me now," Liam says, pointing at me.

I sigh out loud as I pace around my room. Rain begins to pitter-patter down the windows, the sky growing as dark as my mood. "If I get expelled, Dad won't accept that."

"You're right about that." He rolls his eyes. "But you could've told him the truth."

I stop and yell, "Told him what? That I was trying to play the knight in shining armor?" I laugh at how stupid I sound. "No, that's dumb."

"And unbelievable," my brother adds. "But you did it for the right reasons."

64

"Screw what's right," I say, and I point at Liam. "And fuck you for telling Dad about that girl in my room."

He holds up his hands. "Hey now, that wasn't me."

"Who the fuck else could it have been?"

He shrugs. "I don't know, but I wasn't the only one inside the house that day."

"And I'm supposed to believe your word? Give me one good reason."

"I'm your brother," he replies. "There's your reason."

"Yeah, no," I scoff. "You've got to give me something better than that."

He gets up from the bed and walks toward me, broadening his shoulders. "Don't be stupid." He places a hand on my shoulder. "I care about you. I want you to be okay."

My nostrils flare as I look at him, but all I see is truthfulness, and it pisses me off.

Why is he still so fucking nice to me? Is this all just to prove he's the better brother? The one who will take over the company while I'm lying in a ditch somewhere?

"Don't," Liam suddenly says. "Whatever you're thinking, don't."

"You're always so fucking nice, and I hate it."

He plants his forehead against mine, forcing me to stay. "Don't let Father get to you. Whatever he tells you, don't let him get into your mind. Listen to me, Luca. We're better than this. We're brothers."

"While you take over Dad's business and stab me in the

65

back."

He grabs my neck. "I would never fucking do that. Never. Promise on our father's life."

I scoff, "You'd kill him to prove a point?"

"If that's what it takes to prove my loyalty to you as a brother, I would." He strengthens his grip. "Believe me, Luca. And don't let them fucking pit us against each other. If we go down, we go down together."

I nod a few times even though I don't feel the same way.

"You got it?"

I nod again, letting it sink in slowly.

"I'm always going to be honest with you. Straight up," Liam says. "And you know why? Because I love you."

I snort.

"I mean it."

"I know," I reply.

He nods and then slowly releases me from his grip. But his hand is still on my shoulder, and he looks me deep in the eye as he says, "I know you have a thing for Jill, but you have to stop."

I stare at him in confusion with my lips parted.

"I'm telling you this as a brother who loves you, okay?" Liam says.

My lip begins to twitch. "Why?"

"You just can't," he says. "Trust me on that."

Can't?

Trust him?

Rage becomes me, and I grab his shirt and shove him up

against the wall. "What are you hiding?"

"I'm not supposed to tell you but—"

"Tell me," I growl in his face.

He rips my hands off his shirt and shoves me away, showing off his bulky chest and muscular arms as he breathes out loud. And I realize then that he doesn't love me. He's just using my only weakness to try to stop me.

"TELL ME!"

Thunder strikes outside.

A menacing shadow looms behind my brother's figure. The shadow of my ruined future.

His eyes lower to the floor like a sad coward. "Mom told me … Jill's supposed to marry me."

My eyes widen.

Thunder booms again, the sound as loud as the beating of my heart.

But I don't wait until the lightning follows to force open the window and jump outside, running straight into the storm.

EIGHT

Jill

I turn off the light in the bathroom and make my way to my room through the long hallways lined with expensive paintings and statues that stare back at me, reminding me of how lonely I feel in these vast halls.

I sigh as I clutch my bathrobe tight, but I pause the second I hear my parents' voices coming from their bedroom.

"Are you sure it was the right decision to send them there?"

Holding my breath, I sneak closer and clutch the doorway just out of view.

My father paces around the room. "It's the safest school, you heard Lex. These kids need protection."

"But they're already starting fights," my mother says. "It's only been *one* day."

I close my eyes, trying to listen without reacting, but it's hard.

"They're just trying to find out the pecking order."

"What?" My mother gasps, and so do I. "Honestly, you can't be serious."

"It's natural. And it's good for them. It'll toughen them up."

"They're girls!" My mom is visibly upset, and I hate that.

"*And* the heirs to our company," my father says. "Unless you want to go and make a male heir, this is what we've got."

I frown and sigh away the hurt in my heart. Of course, my father would've rather had boys than girls.

"This is my decision, and I am sticking with it. The girls are staying at that school so they can mingle with the De Voses and prepare for the future."

Prepare for the future?

What does he mean?

"But shouldn't we wait to decide which one of our girls marries that boy? I mean, they're not exactly—"

I can't hear what she says anymore because all I can think of is … *marriage?*

Marry that boy?

Who?

I want to shriek, but I plant a hand against my mouth to stop the sound from escaping.

My father stops pacing. "Hey, did you hear something?"

My eyes widen.

Without thinking, I rush away in the opposite direction, taking the long route to reach my room just to avoid being seen. And I slam the door shut behind me, my mind going a million miles an hour as I stand here breathing against the wood.

I've known it for so long, but I kept denying it, hoping it would go away if I didn't think about it.

But it hasn't.

Ever since we were little kids, the tone was set.

My father decides who we marry.

All this time, I thought the De Voses were merely his associates … but what if one of us is supposed to marry one of theirs?

A shiver runs up and down my spine.

I always thought I wanted this. That I wanted to belong to this family and make them proud. But the mere idea of being married off to *anyone* makes the bile rise in my throat.

I slowly walk away from the door, still staring at it like the fires of hell lie beyond.

I am not an object. My sister is not an object. We deserve better.

We deserve a life of freedom.

The sudden sound of the window on my left being opened makes me swallow a shriek. Climbing into my room … is none other than Luca De Vos.

I take a few steps back, clutching my towel tight as it's

the only thing between him and my naked skin. His eyes roam freely across my body, taking ample time to soak up every inch of my skin, and it instantly makes me want to take a cold shower.

Fuck.

I never really stopped to think about how much of an effect just his gaze has on me. Or that lip he just bit while looking me up and down like some tasty piece of meat he wants to devour.

"W-What are y-you doing here?" I stutter, completely losing it because this guy is in my room, and I'm not wearing anything but a skimpy towel.

He runs his hand through his wet hair and pushes it back, and it used to make me think he was arrogant, but now? Now all I see is just how muscular and veiny his arm is, and just how wet his shirt is as it reveals all the thick abs underneath, and …

Oh my God, why am I thinking about Luca like that?

"I wanted to see you," he says.

See … me?

His tongue darts out to wet his lips as his eyes shoot up and down my thin towel again.

Is this thing see-through? Fuck, I hope not.

I still walk back slowly until I bump into the wall and realize there is only one way out … the door. But the second I take a glance, he's right there, blocking my only path out.

"Don't be scared." He raises a hand. "I just want to talk."

"Couldn't you ring the doorbell?" I ask, clearing my throat as he stalks closer.

His face darkens. "No. Your parents can't know I'm here."

My eyes widen. "Why?"

"You know why," he says through gritted teeth. "Same reason mine can't find out."

My lips part in shock.

Does he know too?

"I'm not what they want me to be. I'm not the perfect boy who obeys their every request," he says.

"I'm the same way," I reply. I don't know why I say it or why I even care.

"I know." A lopsided smile forms on his face as he comes closer and closer. Every step he takes makes my breath falter more and more.

He swipes away more rain from his face, brushing his hair aside. A few bruises appear underneath, bruises I don't recognize from the fight at school. Did someone else hit him?

I frown. "What happened?"

Instinctively, my hand inches closer to his face, to the bruise on his cheek. But the second the tip of my finger touches his skin, he grabs my wrist and pins it to the wall behind me, planting his other hand on the wall to trap me inside.

"You."

The word comes out in a single breath, but its power

doesn't evade me. He's so close I can almost feel his rage. He leans in closer, almost as if he's smelling me, and the thought alone makes my breath hitch in my throat.

"I *hate* … you."

My face contorts.

How could he say that?

"Is that what you came here to tell me?" I scoff, feeling tears well up in my eyes. "Get out."

His lip curls up. "Make me."

I shove him with one hand, but he doesn't budge. Again. And again. But no matter how hard I push, I can't even make him move an inch away from me.

"What do you want?" I say, my eyes still unable to look away from the droplets running down Luca's chiseled chest visible through his shirt.

His dark eyes lower to my chest, almost piercing right through before peering back up into mine. "You."

Anger swirls through my body. "I didn't do anyth—"

I can't finish my sentence.

Because his hot lips are on mine.

Consuming me whole.

And I can't fucking breathe.

Luca De Vos … is kissing *me*? But why?

I don't understand. He said he hated me. He's continuously bullied me, pushed me, threatened me, laughed at me.

But now his lips are on mine, claiming me in a way I never thought anyone could. And for some reason, I can't stop him. My whole body grows numb from the feel of his lips smashing onto mine, his tongue coaxing them to part, followed by a groan that sets my body on fire.

His hand moves from the wall to my waist, his body pressing against mine. The thin piece of towel fabric separating us almost falls off. And I can feel every ridge of his muscles, every inch of his delectable body, and even the bulge protruding from his pants.

Fuck.

What is happening?

When his tongue forces itself between my lips and licks the roof of my mouth, one of his hands slides down my arm while the other slithers between the towel.

In an instant, I bite.

He leans back, his finger moving to his face, touching his bloodied lip. His tongue darts out to lick up the blood while his eyes sparkle with curiosity. "You bit me."

"No shit," I retort. "First, you tell me you hate me, and then you kiss me?"

He bursts out into laughter.

"What's so funny about that?" I quip.

"That you think that's all I feel for you," he says, and he plants both his hands beside my head, still trapping me inside. "That you think I'm going to let my brother win."

My eyes widen. "Win wha—"

He grabs my chin, forcing me to look at him. "I hate you for making me want you so much it makes me hate myself."

His words repeat over and over in my mind.

He hates himself … for wanting me.

Is this the reason he kept taunting me? Pushing me?

He releases me from his grip and lets his hand fall as his hair drapes over his eyes like a shadow hiding all his secrets.

"Do you have any idea what it's like to know the one girl you want only wants your fucking brother?"

I shudder in place, goose bumps scattering on my skin.

All this time … he had a crush on me?

No, that can't be true.

"You called that girl to come to your house while I was there, the one with the—"

"With the what, Jill?"

"Those …" My face turns red at the thought.

"Big tits?" He raises a brow like he's amused he could read my mind, and I hate it.

"She was a distraction. From *you*."

My body is pressed against the wall as any movement will bring me closer to him.

Closer to danger.

Closer to the devil himself.

But now that I've licked the flames of hell, I'm not sure I still want to escape.

These dark eyes of his bore into my soul, and I can't stop looking right back into the depths of depravity. The moment seems to last an eternity.

"I … I …" Words fail me.

He tips up my chin with his index finger and turns my

face so I look straight at him. "You can't ever do anything that will *not* make me want you."

I suck in a ragged breath.

He leans in to whisper. "Believe me, I've tried. Hard. Especially because you seem to fucking want the only one who doesn't want you."

Fuck. I can't say that didn't hurt.

Though I've always known Liam prefers my sister, it's tough hearing it from Luca's mouth.

He starts pacing around the room. "You know, I even got into a fight because of you. And not just one, two." He points at the new bruise. "Courtesy of my father."

His father hit him? That asshole!

"I'm sorry," I reply, approaching him, but he swats my hand away when I try to touch him.

"I don't want your pity," he scoffs. "I just want … *Fuck*!"

He walks off, breaking the spell I was under.

Only now can I breathe, but only for a little while because he's still strolling around my room, headed straight for my bookcase. He picks up the crown lying next to my books, the same crown my sister and I were playing with all those years ago, and puts it on his head, then turns to look at me.

"A crown fit for a prince who will never be king. Ironic."

"I don't understand. You bullied me, said I was ugly," I say.

His brows twitch, and he stalks back to me, crown wobbling on his head while his clothes continue to drip onto my floor. "Sometimes, I lie."

"Why?" I say, as he backs me into the wall again.

"To make it easier for you to hate me."

"But I don't …" I say, almost swallowing the words. "Hate you."

His nostrils flare as he looks up and down between my eyes and my lips, almost like he's contemplating whether to kiss me again.

"You should," he says. "I'm not fucking good for you."

Suddenly, he pulls out that knife again, and my heart rate shoots up to what feels like a million beats per minute. He points the blade at my chest.

"All I do is hurt people. It's what I've been taught. But sometimes, I play with them for fun," he says. "Do you even know how much blood this blade has seen?"

I shake my head.

"Does it scare you?"

Sweat drops roll across my forehead. "You won't hurt me."

He cocks his head, a vicious smirk forming on his face. "No … but something inside me makes me want to do this."

His hand slams into the wall beside my face, still holding the knife. I jolt up and down from the shock, only to freeze the second his other hand slides between my thighs and parts them.

"I want what I can't fucking have," he says, inching up underneath my towel.

Until he hits that spot.

"And it makes me want to kill to have it," he murmurs, his face so close to mine I can feel his breath on my skin.

His fingers start to move up and down my pussy, sliding along my clit and opening like he intends to spread my wetness all over. Because one thing is certain … I am as wet as a goddamn pool. And I don't understand why.

I'm not supposed to like a dangerous guy like him. I'm not supposed to like any of this.

Yet … I can't help but let the moan fall out as my lips part, and my eyes almost roll into the back of my head the second he presses his thumb onto my clit.

"You're so wet for me, Jill," he whispers. "Have you ever been this wet for anyone?"

I shake my head, delirious with need as he keeps circling my most sensitive bits like he knows exactly what he's doing and where he needs to go to make me beg for more.

"Did you ever dream about me the way I dreamed about you?" he murmurs into my ear. "Did you ever come just thinking about me?" His dark eyes slide over to mine, looking straight at me while he toys with my pussy. "Like I've done so many times when thinking about you?"

The shock makes me gasp, but no sound escapes as he covers my mouth with his.

And I can't even fucking move as he claims my mouth and my pussy like they've always belonged to him.

When his lips unlatch from mine, I feel bereft. "I think your pussy is telling me all I need to know."

He shoves a finger inside, making my mouth form an o-shape.

My legs wobble, but when I try to move, he holds the knife out in front of my throat.

"Don't move," he says. "And don't make a sound. Don't want to alert your parents."

I swallow away my anxiety as he toys with me while wearing a vicious, gleeful smile on his face.

"So tight … so perfect," he murmurs, thrusting in and out until I'm moaning and bucking my hips against his fingers. "So desperate for me."

"Don't," I murmur.

"Say it like you mean it," he whispers into my ear, and I feel him smile against my skin. "You can't, can you?"

No. I can't. And I hate it.

I hate that I can't say no to him. That I want whatever it is he's willing to give like a beggar looking for scraps.

But what I hate most of all is that he enjoys it.

He presses his bulge against my body, and I can feel it throb through the fabric of his pants.

Slowly, he slides the knife down my neck, and I quiver from the feel of the cold blade on my skin. He moves it down across the towel and slides it between my crevice. My eyes widen, my veins pumping adrenaline through my body as he traces my pussy with the tip of his knife.

A tear forms in my eye, but I blink it away.

"Are you scared of me, little bunny?"

I shake my head, determined not to show him how fearful I am.

Because he thrives on it.

He lives to see the fear in my eyes.

He pulls it back and spins the blade around so he holds the sharp end. "I might be vicious … but I'm not cruel."

Suddenly, he shoves the back end of the knife in my pussy, and I gasp in shock.

I can't believe it's actually inside me as he thrusts and twists it around.

He's holding the blade, and he doesn't even seem to care about the pain it might cause him.

He leans in to lick my earlobe, making my eyes almost roll into the back of my head. I don't know whether to cry or to moan because of what he's doing to me. Because the way he expertly dives into my pussy with that thing makes me question all my morals … all I ever thought I knew about excitement. This is on a whole new level.

"Moan for me, Bunny, and I might give it to you," he whispers.

I fight it. I fight it so hard, but a moan still slips out of my mouth as he starts flicking my clit while thrusting the handle of the knife inside. He toys with me, knowing exactly where to push to get me to react, and my body is helpless against him.

Even though I should hate him.

Despise him.

Fight him.

Instead, I arch my head to the side as he presses a single, all-consuming kiss on my neck. "Say you want me. Say you only want me," he says, looking up into my eyes.

"I want you," I respond in a completely intoxicated state.

I don't even know what I'm doing or saying.

But I don't want him to stop, even if it's wrong, so wrong.

He pulls out the knife, leaving me bereft as he plants the hand holding the knife on the wall, only to replace the emptiness inside me with his finger.

"See … you like this," he murmurs, feeling me from the inside out.

One finger is inside me while another toys with my clit, and I'm almost on the edge of falling apart.

"Show me what it looks like when you fall apart," he says. "You've done that before, haven't you? Fingered yourself."

I nod in delirium as I'm still being ravaged between my legs.

"Good girl," he says. And for some reason, that makes my whole body zing. "So you know what it feels like to come. Now show me."

I gasp as he ramps up the speed, circling and teasing my clit until my knees begin to buckle under me.

"That's it, Bunny … Give me your orgasm."

Fuck.

I can't stop.

A moan slips out as my pussy convulses, my whole body shaking as I almost sink down against the wall. But Luca holds me steady and in place, his eyes roaming across my face and body. The knife comes closer until the tip touches my chest, and he gently slides it across like a warning. A threat.

"Don't tell anyone about this. Ever."

I swallow. Hard.

I can't even protest, no matter how hard I want to.

He stole something from me no other boy has ever taken.

My first.

My first kiss.

My first touch.

My first orgasm.

Because when he asked me if I had touched myself ... I lied.

I haven't.

My mother told me not to. She said it was for grown-ups, and I believed her.

I couldn't imagine what it would be like.

But this ... I never expected this.

And especially not with this boy ...

I always told myself I would give all of it to Liam.

Fuck.

I bite my lip, trying to stop the anger from spilling out as Luca still has a knife pointed right at my heart, and I don't want to endanger myself.

"So this was all just a game to you?" I say. "I'm just another girl you can conquer?"

He draws a heart with the knife, right where my heart truly lies, ending it with a soft puncture to make me bleed.

"I've bled for you, Jill," he says, touching the wound on his head. "It's only fair you do the same for me."

I can't believe this.

"Get out," I hiss, tears welling up in my eyes. I clutch my towel so it doesn't fall after everything that just happened. I don't want to embarrass myself any further.

He takes the crown off his head and places it on my head instead. "My parents are right. This crown doesn't look good on me." I frown as he puts his knife back into his pocket and takes a few steps back. "But I'm glad I got the first taste."

The first taste? Of what? Me?

"What the hell does that mean?" I say.

He brings his fingers to his mouth and takes a lick, the grumbling noise that follows making me all the more aware of my own excitement for him.

When he's done, he says, "They chose *you*. Not Jasmine."

My pupils dilate, and my jaw drops. "What? When? Who told you?"

He keeps backing away like he doesn't want me to get close.

"Liam," he answers, grinding his teeth as he moves back

to the window.

I run to the window just as he's about to take off, the crown tumbling off my head. "Wait, what did he tell you?" I yell as Luca is on his way back down using the balcony.

He jumps down and looks up. "You're supposed to marry *him*."

And he runs off, leaving me with a goddamn tornado of emotions swallowing me up from the inside out.

NINE

Jill

I quickly dress and hopped into one of my dad's cars. I know I'm not supposed to drive by myself, but I can't stay here and wait.

Within minutes, I'm right in front of their giant mansion. I don't know if Luca is here, but that's the least of my problems right now.

Jumping out, I lock the car before going to the side entrance in the yard. I can easily avoid the one camera on that side and climb over the gate.

When I'm over, I pat down my clothes, go to the side of the house, pick up some pebbles from the path, and throw them at Liam's window.

After a while, he opens it up and stares down. The

second he sees me, a smile appears on his face.

"Hey, what are you doing here?" he asks. "How did you get in?"

"The side gate," I respond. "Jumped over." I blink away the raindrops. "I think we need to talk."

He frowns and licks his lips. "Hold on, I'll come down."

He shuts the window again and moves away. The light turns off. After a while, the back door opens, and he walks out into the yard.

"C'mon," he says, holding out his hand. "I'll take you to a safe spot."

"Safe?" I mutter.

"Yeah, if my parents find out you're here, there will be hell to pay."

Something about that statement brings goose bumps to my body.

"Besides, I don't like standing out in the pouring rain."

That's true.

"Up here," he says, pointing at a wooden house in the big tree in the garden.

I was always forbidden from entering when we were little kids. But I guess everyone grows up someday.

I gulp down the nerves as I follow Liam upstairs, and we enter the tiny tree house. It can only fit two or three people at once, and our feet stick out from the door. But it'll do as a temporary hideout.

From here, we can see the busy streets of the city in the distance, car lights flickering everywhere. Sirens blare in the distance, a comforting sound in the darkness of the night in the big city. The only light all the way up here comes from the small lamp hanging from the back door porch, and it's quite cozy in here. But definitely cold. I shiver in place.

"Are you cold?" Liam asks. "Here."

He grabs a soft blanket lying on the floor of the tree house and wraps it around me. "It's not much, but it's all we have. If I knew you were coming, I would've come prepared."

I chuckle. "It's fine. Thank you."

The blanket smells like him. Familiar. Warm. Gentle.

"So, you wanted to talk?" he asks.

I look at him, and the honest kindheartedness reflected in his eyes is something else to witness. Especially compared to the darkness in Luca's. They're complete opposites in every way.

"Yeah." I clutch the blanket tightly. "Luca told me something important so I thought I'd go straight to the source."

"Luca?"

"Yeah, he … came to my house." I gulp back the memories floating to the surface. I don't intend to tell anyone, let alone Liam, about what happened in my room. I'm already mortified enough as it is.

Liam's face darkens. "He told you about the marriage thing, didn't he?" His whole body tenses up. "Yeah, I've known for a while now, but I shouldn't have told him."

"Why not?" I look up into his eyes, but all he does is

look away.

"My parents don't want him to know yet. They fear it'll make him lash out."

"I see …"

"Didn't your parents let you know?" he asks, suddenly looking my way.

I shake my head. "No one ever tells me anything until after the fact."

He snorts. "Imagine finding out you're marrying on your wedding day."

I laugh, but it's not at all funny. "Exactly."

"Not that we're getting married. Yet." He looks at my hand like there's already a ring on it.

"Are you … happy about that?" I ask, my heart fluttering in my chest.

He rubs his lips and looks out into the distance again. There's also a distance between us that I don't know how to describe, but it doesn't feel right.

"It's so quick. I thought I'd have more time," he says. "I thought …"

"What?" I lean in so I can look into his eyes.

"Nothing," he says, smiling. "It's fine. I know my responsibilities."

"You feel like you're missing out," I fill in for him.

"Right," he replies. "That's just it. I wanted so much more. I wanted to travel. See the world. Experience things. But now that our parents have decided, it means we'll be steamrolled into the business so we can take it over one day."

"But it doesn't make sense to me why they would pick me," I reply. "Jasmine has always shown more interest in the business side of things. All I wanted to do was—"

"Escape," Liam interjects with a smile on his face, and it makes me blush.

We both laugh a little and look away for a second. But after a few seconds, his hand threads through mine, and it feels so good that it feels like my heart was lit on fire.

"I guess we have no choice then," I say.

I don't want to appear like I'm okay with our parents forcing this on us, but at the same time, this has always been my dream. I always wanted to marry Liam.

But when I look at him now, his eyes show nothing but solemnness, and it twists at my insides.

"They just pick whoever they prefer. No choice for us whatsoever," he mutters.

I can't help but feel overwhelmed with all of this.

I knew it was coming for a long time … but I never imagined our parents would pick him and me. That I'd be the one to marry Liam. Even though he wants nothing more than to run away.

And he's right. Running away would solve all our problems. We wouldn't have to be forced to marry, and Liam would be able to see the world. And maybe, just maybe, if I went with him, he'd finally fall for me. For real. Not in a forced way.

"We could run away," I say.

He snorts. "What, for real?"

"Why not?" I shrug.

"Our parents would never let that happen," he replies. "Like you said, we have no choice."

I place my head on his shoulder, sighing. "Would you have wanted one?"

"Of course. Everybody does."

"Who would you have picked?"

I close my eyes, knowing I'm not ready for the answer.

Because deep down, I know what he really wants.

Who he'd really choose.

And it isn't me.

"Hey," Liam says, and he turns to me.

I lean up again and blink away a single tear from my eye. He grabs my face and makes me look at him.

"Just because we had different ideas or wants doesn't mean it can't still work out," he says.

"You want Jas—"

He places a finger on my lips.

He closes the gap between us. His face is so close, and my heart begins to race.

"Let me try something," he murmurs, still clutching my face.

And as he closes his eyes, he comes closer, and closer, and closer, and softly plants his lips on mine.

I've waited for this moment since forever.

Wishing upon a star to make it happen.

Liam's kissing me. A feeling that should leave a lasting

imprint on me.

His mouth is warm and sultry against mine.

But the longer he kisses me, the more I realize … I feel nothing.

After a while, he leans back, my lips still red and buzzing from the kiss.

I should be jumping up and down with excitement. Instead, I just sit there, dazed. Completely and utterly confused.

What just happened?

"Did that … do anything for you?" he murmurs.

I lick my lips, afraid to answer.

I don't want this to be the truth.

"Wait, let me try," I say in a moment of impulsiveness, and I smash my lips on his, clutching his face.

I've never kissed a guy so aggressively, but the harder I kiss him, the more it feels vapid.

And the more I begin to see Luca in front of me, kissing me instead.

I tear my lips away from Liam, frowning, angry with myself.

"Why doesn't it work?"

Liam sighs. "I'm sorry. I tried. I just feel …"

"Nothing," I fill in for him.

It hurts.

It hurts because it's exactly what I feel when I kiss him, when I expected so much more.

And I can't help but wonder … would it have been like

this if Luca hadn't stolen my first kiss?

"What the fuck?!"

Luca's distraught voice makes me turn around and look down. He's right there, on the grass, staring up at us with a kind of rage in his eyes that I've never witnessed before.

Oh, God.

TEN

Jill

"You're kissing *him*?!" Luca yells.

Liam holds out his hand. "Luca, stop. You'll wake Dad."

"I don't fucking care!" he yells. "I hope he beats your ass like he did mine." He spits on the ground. "Come the fuck down and face me, you fucking coward."

"Jesus, calm down," Liam says. "It was just a kiss."

"Just a kiss?!" Luca growls, and then he suddenly looks at me. "You … Out of all the things you could've done, this is what you chose?"

He tears off his wet shirt, showing off all the abs underneath and the v-line leading into his pants, and I find it hard not to stare. He fishes his knife from his pocket and draws a heart on his chest, puncturing it right on the spot where he punctured mine, letting the blood roll.

I know what it means ... and I know this is a warning only meant for me.

And it makes my heart drop into my shoes.

I know he saw us kissing, but I'm not sorry. I needed to know the truth.

Why does he even care?

Luca's lips barely part as he sneers at me, "I fucking hate you to death."

"Oh fuck you, Luca. Now you've gone too far." Liam suddenly gets up and jumps down out of the tree house without ever touching the steps. Still, he lands without a scratch, and when he broadens his shoulders, he looks menacingly strong.

The rain begins to pour again as I watch the two having a standoff. Luca clutches his knife while Liam shows off his muscles, and it terrifies me beyond belief to know these two are about to fight.

"All this time, I've tried to keep you from destroying your own goddamn life, and for what?" Liam shouts. "So you can go around and bully girls into hating your guts?"

Luca approaches menacingly with a darkness in his face I've never seen before. "You've got it all wrong, Liam," he hisses, pulling out his knife. "*You* betrayed me."

"You betrayed yourself by behaving like this. And our parents," Liam replies.

"Fuck Mom and Dad," Luca spits. "They chose you, not me."

"So what are you going to do? Cut me?" Liam asks. When Liam opens his arms, my eyes widen. "Go ahead."

"No!" I yell, climbing down the stairs as fast as I can even though it's pouring outside. I run in front of Liam and block him with my arms. "Don't. Please stop, Luca."

His whole face contorts like he can't stand the sight of me, and it hurts. "You choose him? Over me?"

I shake my head, droplets running over my cheeks as I stare at Luca with disbelief, pleading with my eyes to make him stop. "Can't we talk this out?"

His lips twitch as droplets pitter-patter down his chin. "No. Every word from your mouth is poison."

He might as well jam that knife into my heart.

"Get out of my way," he says through gritted teeth.

"No," I reply in a moment of pure, insane courage. "He's your brother, Luca."

"I don't care," he growls, and he suddenly marches straight at me with the knife firmly clutched in his hand.

In a single move, Liam pushes me aside, swooping me out of harm's way, and I fall onto the grass. The harsh landing knocks the air out of my lungs, but when I turn around and see Luca attacking Liam, I still manage to release a squeal.

"Stop, Luca!" Liam yells, trying to fend off Luca, who keeps swiping the knife around like it's a damn sword. "We're brothers!"

"You're not my fucking brother anymore!" Luca yells back, shoving Liam so hard that he has a hard time fighting him off.

Liam might have the physical upper hand, but Luca's knife puts them on the same level of strength, and I don't know who's going to win. I don't want to choose. I don't want them to fight.

It's all my fucking fault.

If I hadn't come here, none of this would've happened.

Tears well up in my eyes, but I push them back and crawl up from the ground. Without thinking, I tear Liam away from Luca's grasp, tugging him with me.

"Let me go," Liam growls at me.

"No. You're coming with me," I reply. "Now."

"Where are you going, Liam?" Luca jests. "Scared I might give you a little cut?"

"This isn't over yet!" Liam barks back.

"C'mon then, fight me, coward," Luca yells back.

Liam tries to shake me off, but I refuse to let him ditch me. Not this fucking time. I stand right in front of him and slap him in the face. "Stop. Now. He could kill you."

"I don't fucking care," Liam says in a fit of rage.

I grab his chin. "But I do."

I look into his eyes, and then it slowly begins to dawn on him.

We're supposed to get married. Our parents expect us to.

But right now … I want nothing more than to run away. Together.

So I grab his hand and coil my fingers through his and

run toward my father's car.

"Jump in," I tell him, and he gets into the passenger's seat while I hop behind the wheel.

"Where are we going?" Liam asks as he straps himself in.

"JILL!" Luca's voice echoes through the streets. "DON'T YOU FUCKING RUN AWAY FROM ME!"

He's right there in my rearview mirror. Fuck.

I don't even answer before I hit the gas and swerve onto the street.

I don't know where I'm going. All I know is that we need to get out of here. Now.

So I ignore the red light in front of me and drive as fast as I can through the city, all along the outer banks until we're far away enough that I can breathe again.

"What are you doing, Jill?" Liam asks.

"I don't know," I say, clutching the steering wheel so hard I feel like I might break it. "But he was about to kill you, and I had to do something."

"I won't let that punk kill me," Liam says, swiping away some of the rain off his forehead. "Jill, you gotta go back."

"What?" I scoff, looking his way. "No, no way am I going back to that lunatic."

"He's not a lunatic. He's my brother," Liam says.

Even though Luca just threatened him with a knife, he still means something to Liam. How can Liam be so kind after all of that?

"He tried to hurt us both," I retort.

"Yeah, well … we hurt him first," Liam says, licking his lips. "He saw us."

A blush creeps onto my cheeks, so I hide my face behind my hair, afraid he'll see. That kiss … should've meant the world. Instead, it did nothing for my heart and ruined everything else.

Fuck.

What do we do now? Where do we go from here?

Luca is surely waiting for us to come back.

And if not … his parents will find out in no time, along with mine.

Either way, we're fucked.

I look out at the boulevard we're driving on, wishing I could just drive off into the sunset with him.

"We should go back," Liam says. "Maybe he's cooled down a little."

The rain still slams down onto the roof, the sky only darkening further. Thunder is encroaching us from all sides, and the silence before the lightning strikes brings goose bumps to my arms.

"Jill," Liam says with a stern voice.

I bite my lip and frown as I look ahead at the swaying palm trees along the boulevard. "No."

"Jill," he growls, his voice almost as loud as the thunderstorm outside. "Turn around."

"It's not safe."

"That's fucking life," he replies.

"So?" I look at him. "I'm just supposed to let him knife

you?"

"You think he's the first to have tried?" He raises his shirt, showing a part of his delectable muscles but also the scars that cover them, and my eyes are glued to his skin.

"Oh my …"

God.

"How did that …?"

"Business. You know the type our parents do," he responds.

And something about that makes my skin crawl.

"I'll fight it out with him, brother to brother," Liam says.

"But what if you lose?" I ask, barely paying attention to the road anymore.

"Then I'll lose, and he gets what he wants …"

The way he looks at me with those beautiful eyes of his undoes me.

There is no darkness to be found.

Until he says the word, "You."

My skin erupts into goose bumps.

Suddenly, lightning strikes right in front of us, and it disorients me so much that I shriek and turn the wheel away from the blast. Off the road. Into the railing.

The car flies up and tumbles in the air several times.

I see stars all around me as the sound of twisting metal and thunder in the sky mingle into complete and utter destruction.

One. Two. Three seconds.

SPLASH!

I don't even see the water before we hit it, the harsh landing knocking me forward and then backward against my seat, knocking me out for a few seconds.

When I come to again, the car is filling up with water … and Liam is still right beside me, out cold.

Oh fuck. Oh fuck. Oh fuck!

I frantically try to undo my belt as the water begins to rise. The car is sinking into the river, and I can't fucking get out. I jerk the door, but the lock is sealed tight from the water trying to get in.

"Fuck, fuck, fuck!" I shove Liam and slap him a few times, but he doesn't wake up. "Liam!"

There's a bloody wound on the back of his head.

Panic swirls in my veins.

"Liam, wake up!" I pull back his belt buckle and try to get him to wake up, but nothing I do is working.

The water is rising so quickly that I'm shivering like crazy.

Still, I gather all my strength and kick at the window, trying to get it to break, but nothing seems to work.

"Goddammit!" I squeal.

This can't be how we die. It just can't be.

I have so much life left in me. So much to do, so much to see.

I wanted to travel the world. Feel free as a bird.

And now the water threatens to take that all away.

It's almost up to my neck now, and I'm freaking out, not

knowing what to do. I look behind me, but I don't see anything, nor beneath me. So I inhale a deep breath and go under, searching for something I can use to break the glass.

Finally, I find the emergency hammer.

The water has gotten to the roof. There's no more air to breathe.

The car is sinking so fast that all the light from the surface is disappearing fast.

I have to hurry.

I hold out the hammer, and ram it as hard as I can at the window. It breaks, and I kick it one last time to move the shards out of the way.

I try to push Liam up, but it's no use. He's far too heavy for me.

My lungs constrict with the need to breathe, but there is no air.

Fuck!

I swim away from him, hoping I can go get him from the other side.

But I'm running out of oxygen. Energy. Life.

No!

I can't stop my body from sucking in water through my mouth and it feels like shards in my lungs.

I keep swimming, fighting against the water, but it's no use.

The more I struggle, the more I lose.

The more I feel myself fading away …

Into oblivion.

ELEVEN

LUCA

My knife is still stinging me in my pocket, but it doesn't even fucking faze me anymore. I'm just staring at the glass of water our butler gave me. The one I haven't touched.

Because my parents are currently crying in the fucking bathroom.

And my mother's screeching cries go through marrow and bone.

"Sir ... do you want me to fetch you some new clothes?"

I turn away, not wanting to even look at him. "No."

My mother's wails fill the house, and I can't fucking stand it.

I get up from my seat and go to the window to stare out at the dark clouds. I always thought the clouds in my own heart were darker than I ever saw them out there. But not tonight.

"Sir," our driver says as he steps inside. "The car is ready."

I throw him a glance and nod. "Go tell my parents. I'll wait in the car."

Thirty minutes later, we're walking into the hospital, my father clutching my mother as she struggles to walk, while I slouch behind them like a damn zombie.

"Follow me, please," one of the nurses who greeted us at the entrance says.

We step into an elevator, where my mother's soft sobs slowly eat away at my heart. Still, I ignore the sting because from here on out, everything will only get darker. Fast.

My parents step out of the elevator, my father clutching my mother tight so she doesn't collapse. Because where we're going, there is no happiness.

Only death.

***

Jill

When my eyes finally open, I feel like I've been asleep for hours, but I'm not rested at all. Machines bleep all around me as I blink away the crustiness. My mouth feels dry, and when I try to speak, all that comes out is a hoarse croak.

"Jill?" My mother's warm voice makes my heart jump.

"Mom," I mutter, tears welling up in my eyes.

I'm alive. I'm alive? How?

"Oh, Jill." Jasmine immediately jumps up from her seat to fall into my lap and cry. "I was so worried about you."

I don't know what to do, so I just hug her even though my entire body hurts.

I look around to try to get my bearings. There are white walls all around me, with a painting of a flower on the wall, and a small kitchenette in the corner, while I'm lying in the only bed in this room … a hospital bed.

"For a second there, we thought we'd lost you," my mother says, grabbing my hand.

Even my father comes to sit close to me. "What you did was very dangerous, Jill. You should be happy we have the very best care in this hospital, or you might not have made it out alive."

Dangerous.

My eyes widen as everything that happened comes flooding back in. The fight between Luca and Liam. Driving off with the car. Toppling over straight into the water. Drowning.

And a body still sitting there in the passenger's seat while the car sinks to the bottom.

I sit up straight in bed, ripping all the wires from my body. "Liam!"

My mother pushes me back down. "Don't get up, Jill.

You're not healed enough yet."

But I don't care what she says. "Liam, where's Liam?!"

"Shhh …" Jasmine tries to shush me even though I can see the hurt in her eyes. "You have to calm down and focus on yourself right now."

"But Liam …!" I retort, but my father's stern eyes force me to shut up.

"You should not have stolen my car in the state you were in, Jill," my father says, clutching my bed railing.

I frown. "What state?"

My mother crosses her arms too now. "Jill, even though we're glad you're okay," she says, sighing, "your father and I are still angry with you for what you did."

"But … But I just wanted to get us to safety, and—"

"Safety?" my father scoffs. "There was a fucking storm outside, and you decided to take my car and drive it off a cliff!"

"Hugo." My mother places a hand on his chest. "She's still our child."

He swats her hand away. "I don't care. She needs to hear this."

"Hear what?" I look at both of them, but neither of them seems to want to answer me. When I turn my head to Jasmine, even she refuses to answer. What's going on?

"I didn't mean for it to happen. I—"

"Jill. We know the truth," my father interjects. "You can't talk your way out of this one."

"What?" I'm thoroughly confused now. "Who told

you?"

Footsteps are audible outside my room, and we all turn to look up when someone appears in the doorway.

But the dark eyes that connect with mine send a chill down my spine.

Luca.

His brown hair falls over his face like a curtain to hide the spite, and it makes me forget my parents are even here.

Of course it was him.

Of course he told them everything that happened.

"Luca," my mother says. "Thank you so much for coming."

"I'm not here for you, ma'am," Luca says, eyeing me down so much that it makes me want to tug this blanket over my head and pretend I don't exist.

"Of course," my mother says, throwing in a lukewarm smile. "Your parents, are they here too?"

More footsteps are audible, the click-clacking sound sending my heartbeat into overdrive. And the second they show their faces, I feel like I might as well prepare my own burial.

Silence fills the room as they look at me first and then my parents.

"Baas," his father says.

"De Vos," mine responds.

The air is filled with electricity. Not the empowering kind, but the kind that predicts war.

"So … Jill is alive," Lex sneers in an unimpressed

manner.

As my father flicks his eyes at Jasmine, she steps away from my bed in obedience.

"We're very lucky," my mother replies with a warm smile in an attempt to lighten the mood.

"You call that luck?" Lex retorts.

I frown, feeling terribly confused as I look at both my parents, who are standing up with fists balled like they're ready to fight. "What's happened? What's going on?" I ask. "And where's Liam?"

"Haven't you heard?" Luca says, his lip curling down viciously. "Liam is dead."

My heart stops right there and then.

Oh God.

Liam.

Liam is … dead?

No, it can't be.

"No," I say, shaking my head. "He was right there."

"Where you left him, in the water, trapped in his seat," Luca says.

Anne approaches me and stares me down.

SLAP!

The sting of her hand on my cheek takes a while to register.

My mother steps in and grabs her wrist.

"Don't you touch my daughter."

They have a standoff, eyeing each other down before Anne finally retracts her hand.

I can still feel her hand on my cheek as the red mark begins to glow, but it doesn't faze me.

"She deserved that. And plenty more," Anne spits, fighting the tears.

She's right. I do.

I'm broken. Shattered into a million bits. That's how I feel.

And no amount of repairing my body here in this hospital bed will fix the destroyed remains of the hearts inside this room.

I killed him.

I killed Liam.

I drove that car straight into the storm.

Straight into the water ...

Tears well up in my eyes, and I can't keep them from running down my cheeks.

"Is he really dead?" I mutter.

"You tell me, girl," Lex says, throwing me a deadly glare. "Because they can't fucking find my son's body."

"And now they've declared him dead," his mother adds, unable to keep the tears at bay.

Oh, God.

He's really gone. Down there in the deep, all alone.

And he begged me to go back.

I bury my face in my hands. "I'm sorry," I mutter. "I'm so sorry."

"You should be," Luca spits. "You killed my brother."

I wish more than anything that I could take it back.

That I could've stopped myself from losing control over the car. "I didn't mean for it to happen."

"But it did," Lex replies, his anger taking over his grief.

"I will never have my son back," Anne says, blinking away the tears with the fury of a scorned woman.

Lex throws my father a look. "And someone has to pay the price."

What? Pay the price? How?

I can't exchange my life for his even though I wish more than anything that I could.

He deserved so much more from the life he was given. And I took it all away from him.

"You will hear from us." With a final warning, Lex and Anne De Vos leave the room.

Only Luca remains, staring me down from the doorway, the spot he hasn't left since the second he stepped in.

"I told you, you shouldn't have run away from me," he says.

Through the tears, I scream, "Get out!"

"Jill!" my mother scoffs at me.

But I pay her no attention as my gaze locks with Luca.

Because he knows exactly why all of this happened.

Why I dragged Liam into that car to begin with.

To escape *him*.

"Hope the hospital takes good care of you," Luca says, licking his lips as he turns around to walk out the door. But not without a final glance … and a warning. "You're gonna need it."

TWELVE

Jill

When I'm finally back home from the hospital, I go straight to my room and lock the door. I don't come down—not for dinner, or breakfast, or my parents, or school. Nothing.

I'm scared.

Scared of what might happen if I do.

Because that warning didn't come without a cost.

Someone must pay the price for Liam being declared dead.

Me.

I shiver as I hear my parents' footsteps stomp up the stairs. They're headed straight for my room.

I jump away from the door and huddle on my bed

before they slam their fists against the door. I was never this scared before. But I guess sometimes trauma changes a person.

Especially when that trauma is connected to mafia families and their need for revenge.

"Jill? Open the door," my mother says.

I don't respond. I don't know what to say, and I'm terrified I'll say the wrong thing.

"Jill, open this door. This is your last warning," my father says with that stern voice of his that makes my skin crawl.

"No," I reply.

"Jill!" my mother gasps.

"Enough," my father barks. He shoves something into the lock and unlocks it from the outside. They burst inside, furious. "You don't think I keep spare keys to all the doors in my own damn house?"

I swallow away the lump in my throat. "I'm sorry. Please."

My father slams the door shut and then looks at me. "We need to talk."

Oh, God.

Here it is.

The *talk*.

The one I've been trying to avoid. Because I've heard them whisper in the hallways about my punishment. But I don't deserve any of this. I didn't kill Liam on purpose.

"Please, you don't have to do this," I say, shaking my

head.

"Jill ..." my mother mutters. "You know we have to. You're going to have to marry Luca."

"No, he's a monster, don't you see it? He'll destroy me for killing his brother."

But her face remains unmoving.

Did she ever care at all?

"Please ..." I mutter.

My mother simply looks at my father and then turns around. "I'll leave her to you."

"Mom!" I yell, but she ignores me as she walks out and shuts the door behind her.

"Jill." My father commands my attention. "You will marry Luca."

No, no, no, this can't be happening. I was supposed to marry Liam.

"Please, don't force me to do this. You don't know what he's like," I plead with him.

"You did this to yourself, Jill," he rebukes. "You made the decision to jump into that car and drag the son you were supposed to marry straight into his death. You think I wanted this?" He's all up in my face right now, yelling like it hurts him more than it hurts me. "You're *my* daughter, and it is *my* job to ensure the De Vos family gets what they're owed. This is the price to pay for what you did."

"But it was an accident," I say, but my voice sounds more like that of a mouse. Tiny. As small as I feel right now.

"Every action has a consequence," he replies. "You

made your choice. Now I'm making mine."

"But why? Can't we offer them something else? Money? More power?"

SLAP!

My father's strike to my face doesn't register until the sizzle of pain follows.

"You think money will bring back the dead?" he scoffs.

I shake my head and shove him away, running straight for the window through which Luca once climbed up into my room. Now, more than ever, do I wish I never let him in. Not into my room nor my body. Because those eyes, those fingers, those lips … destroyed everything I ever held dear.

But before I can say anything else, my father has already grabbed my wrists and put cuffs on them. "Don't try anything. It won't work. They're waiting for you."

***

LUCA

The second our car pulls up to her house, my heart begins to palpitate. I sink into my seat and lower the window to watch my parents get out and meet out front with Hugo Baas, who is standing near the road at the edge of their property. They talk for a moment, and then a guard comes closer, pushing someone forward. A girl in a hoodie and tight leggings with her hands shackled behind her back.

My father approaches her and pulls the hoodie down.

Jill's face isn't kind or sweet anymore.

All I see is rage.

And it stirs something inside me that I didn't know existed.

But the second her eyes connect with mine, they turn to shame. And it's almost as if she's pleading with me for this to stop.

As if I ever had a say in this to begin with.

I take a deep breath and look away while my parents finish up whatever business they have with Hugo Baas. When they finally approach the car, she's in their hands, her eyes stained with tears. They push her forward, each step she takes reluctant. Her eyes skittishly move from left to right as though she's contemplating whether or not to run.

She can try, but she won't get far.

As the side door opens, I turn to watch her get shoved in beside me. The door is slammed shut, and we're locked inside the car together. When she finally looks up, our gazes meet, and my dick instantly hardens in my pants from the sight of her bound wrists and teared-up cheeks.

She's right. I am fucked up.

There's a reason my brother was always the favorite of the family. I could never live up to that. But maybe that was only for the better. After all, I'm still here while he's miles deep in the water.

"Are you enjoying this?" she asks.

I raise a brow. "Are you?"

"They're making me marry you, Luca," she replies, ignoring my question. "My life isn't a joke. This isn't funny anymore."

I plant my elbow on the small windowsill in the car and cock my head. "It wasn't funny when you killed my brother either."

Her face contorts. "I didn't kill him."

"He drowned in the water because of your terrible driving skills."

"There was a storm," she says. "And you don't know if he drow—"

"Exactly. There was a storm," I retort. "And you still chose to drive off in your fucking car."

She throws me a damning glare, but when her lips part, no words come out.

It's quiet for a while, and I look outside at my parents, who are still arguing about fuck knows what with Hugo. I don't even care what's going on.

"Please, Luca. Don't let your parents do this," she says.

My nostrils flare as I shift in my seat to look at her, but the pleading gaze in her eyes catches me off guard.

She's never begged before, and I quite honestly love the sound of her voice when she does. I could listen to this for days. Years.

But she deserves everything she gets for killing my brother. For destroying my parents' vision of the future. And if that means she now becomes *my* wife, so fucking be it.

At least now I'll get a chance to prove I'm the better fucking brother.

"Luca, please, I'm begging you," she says.

Is it so bad to be my fucking wife?

"Convince them. Make them take me in as a servant or something."

A servant?

Jill serving us—me—makes my cock twitch. Fuck, that'd be a sight to behold, watching Jill prance around my room in a skimpy outfit just to pick up after me. I'd pay to see that happening.

But it's not. I don't make the fucking rules, and now that my brother is dead, my parents are more on edge than they've ever been before. After all, he was the favorite son … and now all they have left is me.

The fucking reject son who fucks up every chance he gets.

Just because of …

Her.

I jerk my arm away and sneer, "Don't."

"Luca?" Her brows rise but fall immediately after as though she finally realizes who I truly am. "You owe me this."

"I don't owe you anything," I spit back.

"I took Liam with me in the car to escape you," she says, her eyes darkening with every word she speaks. "He died because of *you*."

I fish my knife from my pocket and point it at her, which immediately makes her freeze.

"He died because *you* kissed him," I say through gritted teeth.

She stares me down, unafraid of the knife inching closer and closer to her chest. A single tear forms in her eyes, but she blinks it away.

"So ... that's it? That's the hill you're willing to die on?" she says, her voice fluctuating in tone. "You were the one who told me our parents were going to make us marry."

I look away as a vicious smile appears on my lips. "Guess fate has a funny way to twist things around."

A shocked gasp hitches in her throat, but I don't care.

After a few seconds, she says. "You're a monster."

The words come out in a stone-cold manner, but it doesn't faze me anymore.

I've already accepted who I am. What I'm willing to do to make her mine.

But she ... She holds her head up with a kind of pride that makes me want to slice her open and tear out her heart.

Because if it can't be mine, it won't belong to anyone.

***

Jill

When the car stops, we're at the airport, and my skin begins to crawl at the sight of those planes flying high above our heads as we get out of the car.

My wrists are still bound, and Lex told Luca to keep a careful eye on me so I don't run away.

"Why are we here?" I ask, wondering why we didn't go to their house.

"Because you're getting married," Lex answers, "on the Canary Islands, far away from your meddling parents."

I stop walking. "What now?"

I don't understand. I thought marriage took preparation. Time. This isn't nearly enough to prepare for … him.

Luca passes me and glances at me over his shoulder, licking his bottom lip like a wolf. "Now."

Fuck.

I have to get out.

No matter what.

I have to run.

So I wait until we're inside the big hall and then say, "I have to pee."

Anne sighs. "Really?"

I nod when she looks my way.

"Fine." She waves it off. "Luca, go with her while Lex and I check in the bags."

Luca rolls his eyes but then grabs my arms, which have been hidden underneath a large coat hanging from my shoulders, so no one here knows my wrists are shackled. But people still stare. And it makes him walk more briskly than ever.

He shoves me inside the bathroom and gets in too, closing the door behind us.

I stare at him wide-eyed. "I need to pee."

"Do it then."

"Well, I'm not peeing with you watching," I reply.

"I'm not leaving." He crosses his arms. "So do whatever you want."

My stomach twists so much I feel like I'm about to puke. I have no plan. This was the plan. What am I supposed to do now?

I go into a stall and close the door, but he can still peer underneath it, and it makes me want to freak out. But there's a time and place for everything, and freaking out isn't part of the plan right now.

Think, Jill, think.

I stare down at my pants.

That's when it hits me.

I can't pee without someone pulling down my pants.

"I can't get my pants off," I say.

Luca grumbles, and within seconds, he's torn open the door. His head blocks the only light in this bathroom while he towers above me and stares me down like he could rip out my heart or my clothes … or both.

119

I swallow hard.

"You want me to help you?" he asks.

Fuck. I have to push through now.

I turn around and show him my wrists. "Can you unlock these so I can at least pee?"

"No," he responds.

"I promise I won't run," I reply.

"Of course you won't," he scoffs.

"I can't pee without my hands, Luca. I'm not a man," I say.

When I glance over my shoulder, his tongue darts out to wet his lips. Dammit. "Lucky me."

I roll my eyes. "Really? You're going to use this opportunity to degrade me some more?"

He tilts his head, and a devilish smirk appears on his face. "Bunny ... I'll use any opportunity I can get."

My blood begins to boil. "I'll fucking pee my pants before I let you touch me."

He makes a disgusting face. "Fine," he spits, and he fishes something from his pocket. The key his parents gave him. The one they got from my father.

Just seeing the damn thing makes my pulse race.

"Turn around," he says, and when I do, he grabs my arms and unlocks the shackles.

I rub my sore wrists and breathe a sigh of relief. But that relief quickly evaporates when I hear the metal jingle.

"These babies are going right back on once you're done. Understand?" He holds them out for me to see like they're toys.

Like he enjoys seeing me in this position.

Of course he does.

"Fine," I sneer. "Can I pee now?"

He shrugs. "Hurry up." He leaves the stall again but stays put right outside the door.

Dammit.

How do I get rid of him?

I sigh and lower my pants to make it sound real, and I sit down on the toilet and look up to make sure he isn't sneaking a peek from above the door.

There is only one other thing I know of that might, might make him run.

He may love the blood when he drains it from someone's veins … but there is one kind I'm positive he doesn't understand.

"Uh-oh …" I mutter.

"What?" he snaps.

"I just got my period," I say.

"So?"

"I don't have any sanitary napkins with me," I say. "Can you go get some?"

He doesn't respond but sighs after a while. "Where do I find them?"

"Ask your mom. She'll have one on her for sure," I say.

He grumbles and slams the door with his fist, making me jolt up and down on my seat. "Fine. But stay here. Or there will be hell to pay. Got it?"

"Like I could go anywhere with bloodied pants," I retort.

He grumbles again and then walks away. When I hear the door close, sweat drops roll down my back.

Of course it was all a lie. I'm not on my period. But he doesn't need to know that.

I quickly get off the toilet, pull up my pants, flush, and run out.

I watch Luca walk toward his parents, who are about fifty feet away. He raises his hand and yells their names. When they look this way, our eyes briefly connect.

Anne's eyes widen as her lips part.

But the first thing I do is run.

As fast as I can.

As hard as I can.

As far as my legs will take me.

Through the crowd, I push people aside, heading toward the door on the other side of the building.

I'm running on pure adrenaline now as I shoot through the hallways. When I turn my head to look for just a moment, there he is.

Luca.

And the look on his face is all I need to know to run faster.

Because that rage alone is enough to kill me.

Shit.

No time to think.

No time to ask for help.

Just run, just fucking run!

I push open the door and run out into the open air, and I suck in a breath to remind myself of just how precious freedom really is … because I know it's going to cost me dearly. But anything is better than being forced to marry Luca De Vos.

So I run toward the nearest cab and give him an address, and I hop inside.

Just before Luca exits the door and looks at me like a hawk who's found its prey. His muscular shoulders rise and fall with each ragged breath he takes. He gave it his all to chase me.

And still, he failed.

The car begins to drive as I hear him scream my name, "Jill!"

The sound goes through marrow and bone.

"I will find you!" he yells as the car drives off, and I look at him through the rearview mirror, just like so many other people out on the street wondering what is going on. "You hear me? I'll fucking search the end of the world if I have to!"

The end of the world.

Yeah, that's what it feels like right about now as I blink away the tears.

Abandoned by my family.

Handed over to the enemy.

Destined to run … until he finds me.

THIRTEEN

Jill

"Vijftig euro, meisje," the driver says.

Fifty euros.

I don't have that.

I don't have anything, in fact. Not even my dignity.

I bite my lip, closing my eyes for a second, before I reply, "The guy inside will have your money."

The driver laughs. "Sure, and I'm the fucking queen."

"I swear on my life," I say. "Please. Just let me talk to him, and I'll get you your money. I swear. You can wait here for me."

He narrows his eyes at me but then waves it off. "Fine. Go."

I don't wait for another second and exit the vehicle,

walking into the restaurant in front of me. Van Buren was literally the only place that came to my mind where I felt I'd be relatively safe. For now. My parents will surely come to find me once they find out I ran. I'm not safe with them, nor with anyone else I know at this point.

Even though I'll definitely miss Jasmine more than anything.

I sigh and walk inside. The place is empty as it's the middle of the day, and the restaurant hasn't opened up yet, but I still take a peek inside as I'm sure the staff is already preparing for tonight.

A server notices me, and I quickly pull down my hoodie as she approaches me. "Hey, can I help you?"

"Yeah, I'm looking for Easton. Easton Van Buren," I reply, twiddling my thumbs.

But the way all the warmth seems to evaporate from her face makes me question what I just said.

"Easton?" she mutters.

"Yeah. This is his restaurant, right?" I mutter.

"Yeah, yeah … I'm just … nothing." She clears her throat.

"Tell him Jill Baas wants to talk to him," I add.

"Of course," she says before she walks off into the back behind the bar. The silence that follows makes me all the more aware of my heartbeat ticking right out of my chest.

The second she comes walking back with him, the nerves take over, and I smile like an idiot when Easton appears.

He frowns when he sees me. "Jill? I didn't expect to see you back so soon."

The server looks utterly confused as to why he would know me, but she shrugs and walks off to clean the rest of the tables.

"Mr. Van Buren," I say, but my voice sounds more like a mouse squeak.

Easton approaches me. "What are you doing here? Where's Hugo?" He looks around like he's waiting for my father.

"I ran away from them," I spit out.

His brows furrow even more. "What?" He places a hand on the small of my back. "C'mon. Sit down first."

I pause and say, "I need to pay the driver first. But I don't have any money."

Easton nods and then flicks his fingers at the server. "Pay the driver outside for me."

The server nods and rushes out the door while Easton gently nudges me toward a table. "Tell me what's going on."

I stop and turn around to place my hand on his elbow, looking up into his serious eyes while mine fill with tears. "I need your help," I plead. "Don't tell my parents I'm here, please."

He swallows, visibly shaken by my request. "What happened?"

My breath falters at the thought of having to explain it all, so I keep it simple. "I did something bad, and my parents traded me to the De Vos family. They wanted to force me to

126

marry one of their sons, Luca."

Easton pulls back a chair and beckons me to sit. "How long ago did you escape?"

"An hour ago, sir," I say, staring at the clock.

It feels so much shorter than that.

Like it happened only minutes ago.

"Are they looking for you now?"

I nod. "Please, don't send me back to them, sir."

He reaches across the table and holds out his hand. It's warm and gentle and everything I need right now to make me cry.

"I will do my best to keep you safe, Jill."

"I can't go back. Not to my own family or to the De Vos family," I say. "But I don't have any money or a place to stay."

He looks me in the eyes and says, "I will take care of it."

"I ... I ..." I don't know how to respond.

Can Easton really help me?

I barely know him, apart from some conversations we had while my family was having dinner here. He's a few years older than I am, but he built an empire from the ground up. Maybe this man does know more about the world I come from than he lets on.

Why else would my parents come here so often?

"You can trust me," Easton says, squeezing my hand.

What other choice do I have than to believe him?

"Do you want me to help you?" he asks. "Think carefully about what this means. You won't be able to see

127

your family again. It's too dangerous."

I don't need a second thought. "Yes. Help me."

He sucks in a breath and holds it, his body tensing up. "All right," he says, raising a brow. "But …"

Of course there is always a but.

"But?"

"My help is not for free."

I take in a breath. "I understand that."

I wonder what his price is, though.

"Good. You'll have to work for me."

That … seems stupidly easy compared to what I would have to go through if I had stayed with the De Vos family. If Luca had his way with me.

I smile, shaking my head. "That's all?"

He smiles back in a way that makes me feel welcome. "That's all."

***

Three years later

When the sewing machine stops, I pull out the little dress I made and hold it over the doll. A big grin forms on my face. It fits perfectly.

"Amazing!" Charlotte, Easton's wife, says, snatching it out of my hand to look at it. "I can't believe you made this all by hand." She puts it over the doll until it fits snugly. "Perfect. Just what I was looking for."

"Thank you," I reply.

I always take pride in my work. I never thought I'd end up enjoying making clothes as much as I do, but when Easton told me to get busy with the fabrics he gave me, I never stopped. He probably knew I had a penchant for designing the most extravagant dresses. Though, I doubt he'd realize I'd eventually end up making them for the tiniest of models. And that I'd be working for his wife.

I smile at her. "Do you think the girls will like them?"

"Of course!" Charlotte exclaims, stuffing the doll in a box. She grabs some wrapping paper and covers the box until it looks pretty, sticking on a bow for the final touch. "There. The perfect gift for a kid in need. I'll need plenty more!"

I blush. It's really humbling to know that my work will make someone happy, especially when that someone is a little kid who doesn't have anyone else in the world. I wish I could give them so much more. If I had my family's wealth, it would've all been possible.

I sigh out loud.

At least Easton kept me out of harm's way for so long. It's a miracle my family hasn't found me yet. I even wore a wig in the beginning so no one would recognize me, but now I just cut my own hair short and keep my business outside the house brief.

Easton knows just how to avoid the De Vos and Baas gaze by keeping them so close they'd never suspect him of anything. And it helps that he has spies all over town to tell him when I need to lay low for a while.

"Something the matter?" Charlotte says.

"Oh, nothing," I say, shaking my head. "I was just lost in my own thoughts, that's all."

I look away at the door, where Nick, Easton's most trusted guard, is dutifully guarding the place. Easton never wants Charlotte to go unaccompanied. Not because he doesn't trust her, but because he involves himself with dangerous men who could try something at any time.

Like my father and …

Just the thought of the De Vos family makes my throat clamp up.

"Oh … Of course," Charlotte muses.

"Huh?"

"You like Nick, don't you?"

My eyes widen, and my cheeks turn red. "What? Why would you—"

"Oh, c'mon, I've seen you look at him," she says, winking. "I can tell when something's going on."

"Nothing," I say. "Nothing's going on."

She raises a playful brow. "You sure?"

"I haven't had a boyfriend in forever." I snort.

She gasps. "A boyfriend?" She leans over the table all across the fabrics I need, stopping me from continuing my work. "C'mon, tell me. I wanna know more about your past. How did you end up working for Easton?"

My whole body tenses up. "Well … I …"

She frowns, grabbing my hand. "Hey. I consider you my

friend now. You can tell me anything."

She squeezes gently, just like Easton always did when he wanted to make me feel better, and it moves me to speak up.

"Okay …" I take a deep breath in and out. "Grab a chair then because it's gonna be a long story."

***

After I've told her everything, it takes Charlotte a while to respond. She takes in a deep breath. "Wow."

"Yeah …" I murmur as I grab some new cloth and start cutting it into pieces for the next dress. "It's a lot."

"I'm sorry," she says.

"Oh, don't be. It happened a long time ago," I reply.

"But still," she says. "Can't imagine what it must've been like for you, losing your entire family like that."

I sigh and look away for a moment, still clutching the fabric in my hand. "I do miss them. Sometimes. Mostly my sister." A pang of guilt hits me in the stomach, and I shake my head. "I try not to think of it."

Charlotte grabs my hand. "I'm here for you. If you need me." The way she looks at me makes me tear up, but I swallow it down. "It's okay to be angry. To be sad."

"I know, but it doesn't change anything," I say, shrugging it off. "Besides, Easton kept me safe. I'm very grateful."

I continue sewing, but a part of me still digs in my

memories as I try to picture what Jasmine would look like right now and what she's doing. If she's still involved with our parents' business. If they made her take over. If she's happy...

"I do wonder sometimes how my sister is," I blurt out.

Charlotte looks at me while curling her hair around her finger. "Can't we look her up? What's her name?"

I gaze up at her and put down my stuff, but I don't know what to say.

"I ... I ..."

"It won't do any harm to know, right? They won't find you," she says as she fishes her phone from her pocket and opens a search tab.

"Easton told me to never say the name out loud," I reply. "It could get me in trouble."

I've actually never searched online for any of my family members.

I was terrified.

Terrified of the consequences.

Terrified of what I'd find out.

"I won't tell anyone," Charlotte says, crossing her fingers. "Promise."

I sigh again. "My full name ... is Jill Baas."

I haven't said that name in years.

It feels odd.

And it makes my skin crawl.

"Baas ... hmm ..." Charlotte types on her phone but stops as her eyes widen. "Oh!"

I jump from my seat. "What?"

She turns the phone to me. "Is this her? Jasmine Baas?"

My heart comes to a stop the second I look into the eyes of my own sister.

The one girl I thought I'd never see again.

And it makes tears well up in my eyes.

I nod. "I never got to say goodbye …"

Charlotte's face contorts. "I'm sorry, I didn't want to upset you."

"Can I have a closer look?" I ask.

She hands me her phone. "Of course."

But when I take it, it almost drops from my hand.

My whole body feels numb.

Like I'm not really here.

Because my sister's name and face aren't just online for everyone to find.

The photo on the social media account shows her trying on a wedding dress.

With the caption "Today a Baas. Tomorrow a De Vos."

Oh, God.

"What's wrong?" Charlotte asks. "Your face is turning white."

My lips quiver as I speak. "She's getting married … to the boy who destroyed us."

She frowns. "What?! You mean Luca De Vos?"

I nod as the phone shakes in my hand, rage bubbling to the surface.

They couldn't have me.

Couldn't keep me from running.

From hating him.

So they took my sister instead.

"Fuck," I growl, and I hand her back the phone before I squash it. "I have to go."

"What? Where?" Charlotte asks while I grab all my things and tuck them in my bag.

I don't know where she is right now, but I can find out the wedding date and location if I just search online.

"Don't tell me you're going to try to find her," Charlotte says. "It could be dangerous."

I pull my bag over my shoulder and march toward the door, only throwing her a single glance. "I can't let my sister take the fall for my mistake. I have to save her."

"What if he kills you?" she yells, but it won't stop me.

"He won't," I respond while I open the door to the workshop. "I have something Luca wants. Me."

FOURTEEN

LUCA

When the bride steps inside the room, the smile that I was wearing for my parents dissipates. The small gathering gasps in unison at the beauty marching down the aisle. She looks beautiful in that semi-white, laced dress that tightly fits her body.

Beautiful. Perfect in every way.

But it's not enough to make me smile.

I adjust my bow tie as everybody watches her step forward in those pristine pretty shoes she'll only wear once.

All of it is fleeting, just like this wedding, just like any kind of feelings I once felt.

None of it matters.

The only thing that does is the fact that this is my wedding day. And Jasmine Baas will now officially become Jasmine De Vos.

My wife. My little pet.

A girl simply there to mend the broken relationship between our families. A girl here to satisfy all my wicked needs.

But when I look at her, I feel … nothing.

No excitement. No rage. No lust pulsing through my veins.

None of the things I desire.

This girl isn't the girl I wanted.

But I have her now, so I'll make do.

After all, our families need to keep their dealings going, and I'm the only son left standing to carry the weight of this business on my shoulders. I'm merely a means to an end, just like she is. A gesture of peace, to put a looming war to an end.

But to look at her and know that I'm supposed to spend the rest of my life with a girl who never wanted to be here, who can't even stand the fucking air I breathe, makes me grumble out loud. In front of everyone. And I don't even care.

She rolls her eyes, obviously not interested in whatever it is I'm thinking. The feeling is mutual. She despises me as much as I despise her, but I don't fucking care.

If I can't fucking have what I want, I will take the next best thing.

So I straighten my back and wait until Jasmine is at the altar. She reluctantly offers her hand, and I take it and own it as we step to the front and wait for the moment we say our vows.

I'm hyperaware of the ring in my pocket waiting to be put on her finger.

And when the man who is making our marriage a fact is finally done speaking, we turn to face each other. Her eyes are filled with tears as I lift her veil, but she doesn't even look at me.

It doesn't matter. Once this is all over and she is my wife, I'll *make* her look at me.

"Are you ready to say your vows?" the man in front of the altar asks.

I nod. "We are."

Jasmine doesn't say anything, like a pretty little doll told to shut up.

Exactly what's needed for an exchange like this.

If only my dark heart didn't hunger for more.

More defiance, more hatred, more rage. Because an eager to please submissive like Jasmine is never going to fulfill my depraved needs.

There is only one girl on this entire fucking planet who could …

But she ran and vanished off the face of the earth.

And now that our families have finally come to an agreement, I have to honor my side of the deal, no matter how bitter it makes me.

At least I'll have the fucking crown.

I clear my throat and take out the ring holding out her hand.

Suddenly, the door in the back bursts open, and everyone turns their head, including me.

But when I see who steps inside, I'm the only one whose smile grows bigger and bigger.

Out of all the people to show up to my wedding … I never expected it to be her.

Jill.

"Stop!" she yells, her breathing as ragged as the clothes she's wearing. But her voice … even after all these years, it still lights the fire in my heart.

And the second her eyes connect with mine, I know this is going to be the most amazing wedding I have ever witnessed.

"Jill Baas … how nice of you to finally show your face again," I say, grinning because I can't contain the ecstasy flurrying through my body. "I've missed you."

"Jill?" Jasmine mutters with confusion. Maybe she didn't know Jill was going to show up either. "What are you doing here?"

"Saving you," Jill replies. She steps forward, undeterred by the shocked audience as she looks me dead in the eyes. "Let. Jasmine. Go."

My nostrils twitch from annoyance.

She thinks she can just barge in here and decide what's going to happen? Wrong.

"Give me one good reason," I sneer.

Jasmine throws Jill some looks with her eyes. These sisters have always communicated without saying a single word, and it makes me want to lash out.

I grab Jasmine's arm and push her back so she's behind me, and Jill can no longer speak with her.

"She doesn't deserve this," Jill says.

"She's doing what's best for her family," I retort.

Jill's face darkens. I can tell she takes it personally, and I love the way her hatred for me only seems to grow with every passing second she spends at this damned wedding that's doomed to fail.

"No," Jill says, her voice loud and clear. "Take me instead."

Everyone gasps, including me.

I didn't think this wedding could get any better.

But now … now she's given me the best wedding gift any groom could ever receive.

A second chance at claiming what should always have belonged to me.

And this time … she's not getting away.

To be continued in THE MARRIAGE DEBT!

THANK YOU
FOR READING!

Thank you so much for reading The Wedding Debt. Please leave a review if you enjoyed!

Make sure to order the full length sequel, The Marriage Debt.

Sign up for my newsletter if you want to know exactly when it launches: clarissawild.com/newsletter

I'd love to talk to you! You can find me on Facebook: www.facebook.com/ClarissaWildAuthor, make sure to click LIKE.

You can also join the Fan Club: www.facebook.com/groups/FanClubClarissaWild and talk with other readers!

Enjoyed this book? You could really help out by leaving a review on Amazon and Goodreads. Thank you!

ALSO BY CLARISSA WILD

Dark Romance

The Debt Duet

House of Sin Series

His Duet

Savage Men Series

Delirious Series

Indecent Games Series

The Company Series

FATHER

New Adult Romance

Cruel Boy & Rowdy Boy

Ruin

Fierce Series

Blissful Series

Erotic Romance

Hotel O

Unprofessional Bad Boys Series

The Billionaire's Bet Series

Enflamed Series

Visit Clarissa Wild's website for current titles.

www.clarissawild.com

ABOUT
THE AUTHOR

Clarissa Wild is a New York Times & USA Today Bestselling author with ASD (Asperger's Syndrome), who was born and raised in the Netherlands. She loves to write Dark Romance and Contemporary Romance novels featuring dangerous men and feisty women. Her other loves include her hilarious husband, her cutie pie son, her two crazy but cute dogs, and her ninja cat that sometimes thinks he's a dog too. In her free time, she enjoys watching all sorts of movies, playing video games, and cooking up some delicious meals.

Want to be informed of new releases and special offers? Sign up for Clarissa Wild's newsletter on her website www.clarissawild.com.

Visit Clarissa Wild on Amazon for current titles.

Printed in Great Britain
by Amazon

22639985R00081